THE SUPERNATURAL
SHORT STORIES
OF
SIR WALTER SCOTT

Other books edited by Michael Hayes
THE SUPERNATURAL SHORT STORIES OF ROBERT
LOUIS STEVENSON

THE SUPERNATURAL SHORT STORIES

OF

SIR WALTER SCOTT

Edited with an introduction by Michael Hayes

John Calder

LONDON

THE CALDER COLLECTION

Calder Publications is an imprint of

ONEWORLD CLASSICS LTD
London House
243-253 Lower Mortlake Road
Richmond
Surrey TW9 2LL
United Kingdom
www.oneworldclassics.com

The Supernatural Short Stories of Walter Scott first published by John Calder
(Publishers) Ltd in 1977
This edition published by Calder Publications in 2010
Selection and original material © Michael Hayes 1977, 2010

Printed and bound in Great Britain by CPI Antony Rowe Eastbourne and
Chippenham.

ISBN (HARDBACK): 978-0-7145-4362-8
ISBN (PAPERBACK): 978-0-7145-4363-5

For my sisters
Mary, Christina, Eileen, Veronica
remembering the Villa Rose

CONTENTS

	Page
Introduction	9
The Tapestried Chamber	13
My Aunt Margaret's Mirror	33
Wandering Willie's Tale	75
The Two Drovers	99
The Highland Widow	133
Glossary to *Wandering Willie's Tale*	213

INTRODUCTION

The robust life of olden times, the days of chivalry and mediaeval pageants, the might of the great contrasting with the wretched poverty of the peasant, are all familiar to the readers of Sir Walter Scott's romantic novels. Less well-known are the handful of short stories which—over-shadowed, perhaps, by these historical novels—have suffered an unjust share of obscurity. Scott's great gifts were suited to the large canvas of the epic novel. Yet, the small frame of the short story in no way restricted his talent, but rather refined it.

From an early age, Scott was fascinated by ghostly legends, superstitions, and eldritch lore. So that, right through his novels and short stories there flows an element of the supernatural, handled with skill and discretion.

The Tapestried Chamber is a splendid example of a Georgian ghost story. The simple story-line and the antique setting contrive to give this tale a compelling quality, leaving the reader with the eerie sensation that he has been watching the scenes and characters through a dusty pane of glass.

Alfred, Lord Tennyson admired *The Tapestried Chamber,* but considered *My Aunt Margaret's Mirror* as 'the finest of all ghost or magical stories.' It is an elegant tale of magic which, in spite of the homely personality of the narrator, makes compulsive reading. This story and *The Tapestried Chamber,* originally meant for publication in the *Chronicles of the Canongate,* were rejected by Scott's publisher as unworthy of the author of Waverley. They were published later in *The Keepsake,* 1828.

It was not uncommon for eighteenth century authors to revive a flagging suspense by grafting sub-plots to the main stem of their novels. Scott copies this technique in *Redgauntlet,* by inserting what must be his most accomplished short story, *Wandering Willie's Tale.* Dante Gabriel Rossetti thought it the *best* and, indeed, it must stand among the fifty best short stories in English literature. This tale of diablerie—with more than a hint of satire—is told in scots vernacular, which heightens the strangeness with the powerful, sinewy raciness of everyday speech. Howard Phillips Lovecraft, in his distinguished essay, *Supernatural Horror in Literature,* summed it up perfectly when he wrote, 'the force of the spectral and the diabolic is enhanced by a grotesque homeliness of speech and atmosphere.' To borrow something Robert Louis Stevenson said of himself— if Scott had written nothing else but *Wandering Willie's Tale* he would still have been a writer.

Second sight provides the supernatural element in *The Two Drovers.* From the moment the witch-like Janet warns the drover Robin Oig that 'there is blood on your hand, and it is English blood,' the story is given focus, and there enters a relentless progression of fatal events towards the inevitable fulfilment of the terrible prophecy.

It is probably in *The Highland Widow* that Scott best displays his fascination for the marvellous, reluctantly tempered by a measure of scepticism. His ambivalent attitude is reflected in the way he weaves the supernatural in and out of this gripping story, across the brooding hills and haunted glens, and around the central character, Elspat, whom he justly likens to a heroine of Greek tragedy: the passionate and jealous mother who, pursued by the Fates and the Furies, becomes the unfortunate instrument of her son's doom.

By his own admission, Scott expressed a total lack of interest in the craft of fiction—'Style—I never think about style. I have had regiments of cavalry marching through my head ever since I was fourteen'—and this is obvious in his novels. Storytelling was all important, so that in the grand tapestries of his novels you will find beautiful areas surrounded by threadbare patches. Not so in his short stories; flaws, perhaps—threadbare patches, never. Lord David Cecil accurately observed that 'even around his worst work hovers a hint of careless greatness.'

It is acknowledged that Sir Walter Scott is one of the best known authors in English literature—and one of the least read. Why? G. K. Chesterton's reply to that is memorable: 'It is said that Scott is neglected by modern readers; if so, the matter could be more appropriately described by saying that modern readers are neglected by Providence.'

Michael Hayes

THE TAPESTRIED
CHAMBER

THE TAPESTRIED
CHAMBER

A BOUT the end of the American war, when the officers of
Lord Cornwallis's army, which surrendered at York-
town, and others, who had been made prisoners during the
impolitic and ill-fated controversy, were returning to their
own country to relate their adventures and repose themselves after their fatigues, there was amongst them a general
officer, of the name of Browne—an officer of merit, as well
as a gentleman of high consideration for family and attain-
ments.

Some business had carried General Browne upon a tour
through the western counties, when, in the conclusion of a
morning stage, he found himself in the vicinity of a small
country town, which presented a scene of uncommon
beauty, and of a character peculiarly English.

The little town, with its stately old church, whose tower
bore testimony to the devotion of ages long past, lay amidst
pastures and cornfields of small extent, but bounded and
divided with hedgerow timber of great age and size. There
were few marks of modern improvement. The environs of
the place intimated neither the solitude of decay nor the

bustle of novelty; the houses were old, but in good repair; and the beautiful little river murmured freely on its way to the left of the town, neither restrained by a dam nor bordered by a towing-path.

Upon a gentle eminence, nearly a mile to the southward of the town, were seen, amongst many venerable oaks and tangled thickets, the turrets of a castle as old as the wars of York and Lancaster, but which seemed to have received important alterations during the age of Elizabeth and her successor. It had not been a place of great size; but whatever accommodation it formerly afforded was, it must be supposed, still to be obtained within its walls; at least, such was the inference which General Browne drew from observing the smoke arise merrily from several of the ancient wreathed and carved chimney-stalks. The wall of the park ran alongside of the highway for two or three hundred yards; and through the different points by which the eye found glimpses into the woodland scenery it seemed to be well stocked. Other points of view opened in succession—now a full one of the front of the old castle, and now a side glimpse at its particular towers, the former rich in all the bizarrerie of the Elizabethan school, while the simple and solid strength of other parts of the building seemed to show that they had been raised more for defence than ostentation.

Delighted with the partial glimpses which he obtained of the castle through the woods and glades by which this ancient feudal fortress was surrounded, our military traveller was determined to inquire whether it might not deserve a nearer view, and whether it contained family pictures or other objects of curiosity worthy of a stranger's visit, when, leaving the vicinity of the park, he rolled through a clean and well-paved street and stopped at the door of a well-frequented inn.

Before ordering horses to proceed on his journey, General Browne made inquiries concerning the proprietor of the chateau which had so attracted his admiration, and was equally surprised and pleased at hearing in reply a noble-man named whom we shall call Lord Woodville. How fortunate! Much of Browne's early recollections, both at school and at college, had been connected with young Woodville, whom, by a few questions, he now ascertained to be the same with the owner of this fair domain. He had been raised to the peerage by the decease of his father a few months before, and, as the General learned from the landlord, the term of mourning being ended, was now taking possession of his paternal estate, in the jovial season of merry autumn, accompanied by a select party of friends, to enjoy the sports of a country famous for game.

This was delightful news to our traveller. Frank Woodville had been Browne's fag at Eton, and his chosen intimate at Christ Church; their pleasures and their tasks had been the same; and the honest soldier's heart warmed to find his early friend in possession of so delightful a residence, and of an estate, as the landlord assured him with a nod and a wink, fully adequate to maintain and add to his dignity. Nothing was more natural than that the traveller should suspend a journey which there was nothing to render hurried to pay a visit to an old friend under such agreeable circumstances.

The fresh horses, therefore, had only the brief task of conveying the General's travelling-carriage to Woodville Castle. A porter admitted them at a modern Gothic lodge, built in that style, to correspond with the castle itself, and at the same time rang a bell to give warning of the approach of visitors. Apparently the sound of the bell had suspended the separation of the company, bent on the various amusements of the morning, for, on entering the court of the chateau, several young men were lounging about in their sporting-dresses, looking at and criticising the dogs, which the keepers held in readiness to attend their pastime. As General

Browne alighted, the young lord came to the gate of the hall, and for an instant gazed as at a stranger upon the countenance of his friend, on which war, with its fatigues and its wounds, had made a great alteration. But the uncertainty lasted no longer than till the visitor had spoken, and the hearty greeting which followed was such as can only be exchanged betwixt those who have passed together the merry days of careless boyhood or early youth.

'If I could have formed a wish, my dear Browne,' said Lord Woodville, 'it would have been to have you here, of all men, upon this occasion, which my friends are good enough to hold as a sort of holiday. Do not think you have been unwatched during the years you have been absent from us. I have traced you through your dangers, your triumphs, your misfortunes, and was delighted to see that, whether in victory or defeat, the name of my old friend was always distinguished with applause.'

The General made a suitable reply, and congratulated his friend on his new dignities, and the possession of a place and domain so beautiful.

'Nay, you have seen nothing of it as yet,' said Lord Woodville, 'and I trust you do not mean to leave us till you are better acquainted with it. It is true, I confess, that my present party is pretty large, and the old house, like other places of the kind, does not possess so much accommodation as the extent of the outward walls appears to promise. But we can give you a comfortable old-fashioned room, and I venture to suppose that your campaigns have taught you to be glad of worse quarters.'

The General shrugged his shoulders and laughed. 'I presume,' he said, the worse apartment in your chateau is considerably superior to the old tobacco-cask in which I was fain to take up my night's lodging when I was in the bush, as the Virginians call it, with the light corps. There I lay, like Diogenes himself, so delighted with my covering from the elements that I made a vain attempt to have it rolled in to my next quarters; but my commander for the time would give way to no such luxurious provision, and I took farewell of my beloved cask with tears in my eyes.'

'Well, then, since you do not fear your quarters,' said Lord Woodville, 'you will stay with me a week at least. Of guns, dogs, fishing-rods, flies, and means of sport by sea and land, we have enough and to spare; you cannot pitch on an amusement, but we will find the means of pursuing it. But if you prefer the gun and pointers, I will go with you myself, and see whether you have mended your shooting since you have been amongst the Indians of the back settlements.'

The General gladly accepted his friendly host's proposal in all its points. After a morning of manly exercise, the company met at dinner, where it was the delight of Lord Woodville to conduce to the display of the high properties of his recovered friend, so as to recommend him to his guests, most of whom were persons of distinction. He led General Browne to speak of the scenes he had witnessed; and as every word marked alike the brave officer and the sensible man, who retained possession of his cool judgment under the most imminent dangers, the company, looked upon the soldier with general respect, as on one who had proved himself possessed of an uncommon portion of personal courage—that attribute, of all others, of which everybody desires to be thought possessed.

The day at Woodville Castle ended as usual in such mansions. The hospitality stopped within the limits of good order; music, in which the young lord was a proficient, succeeded to the circulation of the bottle; cards and billiards, for those who preferred such amusements, were in readiness; but the exercise of the morning required early hours, and not long after eleven o'clock the guests began to retire to their several apartments.

The young lord himself conducted his friend, General Browne, to the chamber destined for him, which answered the description he had given of it, being comfortable, but old-fashioned. The bed was of the massive form used in the end of the 17th century, and the curtains of faded silk, heavily trimmed with tarnished gold. But then the sheets, pillows and blankets looked delightful to the campaigner, when he thought of his 'mansion, the cask.' There was an air of gloom in the tapestry hangings which, with their worn-out graces, curtained the walls of the little chamber, and gently undulated as the autumnal breeze found its way through the ancient lattice-window, which pattered and whistled as the air gained entrance. The toilet, too, with its mirror, turbaned, after the manner of the beginning of the century, with a coiffure of murrey-coloured silk, and its hundred strange-shaped boxes, providing for arrangements which had been obsolete for more than fifty years, had an antique, and in so far a melancholy aspect. But nothing could blaze more brightly and cheerfully than the two large wax candles; or if aught could rival them, it was the flaming, bickering fagots in the chimney, that sent at once their gleam and their warmth through the snug apartment, which, notwithstanding the general antiquity of its appearance, was not wanting in the least convenience that modern habits rendered either necessary or desirable.

'This is an old-fashioned sleeping-apartment, General,' said the young lord, 'but I hope you find nothing that makes you envy your old tobacco-cask.'

'I am not particular respecting my lodgings,' replied the General; 'yet were I to make any choice, I would prefer this chamber by many degrees to the gayer and more modern rooms of your family mansion. Believe me, that when I unite its modern air of comfort with its venerable antiquity, and recollect that it is your lordship's property, I shall feel in better quarters here than if I were in the best hotel London could afford.'

'I trust—I have no doubt—that you will find yourself as comfortable as I wish you, my dear General,' said the young nobleman; and once more bidding his guest good-night, he shook him by the hand and withdrew.

The General once more looked round him, and internally congratulating himself on his return to peaceful life, the comforts of which were endeared by the recollection of the hardships and dangers he had lately sustained, undressed himself, and prepared for a luxurious night's rest.

Here, contrary to the custom of this species of tale, we leave the General in possession of his apartment until the next morning.

The company assembled for breakfast at an early hour, but without the appearance of General Browne, who seemed the guest that Lord Woodville was desirous of honouring above all whom his hospitality had assembled around him. He more than once expressed surprise at the General's absence, and at length sent a servant to make inquiry after him. The man brought back information that General Browne had been walking abroad since an early hour of the morning, in defiance of the weather, which was misty and ungenial.

'The custom of a solder,' said the young nobleman to his friends; 'many of them acquire habitual vigilance, and cannot sleep after the early hour at which their duty usually commands them to be alert.'

Yet the explanation which Lord Woodville thus offered to the company seemed hardly satisfactory to his own mind, and it was in a fit of silence and abstraction that he awaited the return of the General. It took place near an hour after the breakfast bell had rung. He looked fatigued and feverish. His hair, the powdering and arrangement of which was at this time one of the most important occupations of a man's whole day, and marked his fashion as much as, in the present time, the tying of a cravat, or the want of one, was dishevelled, uncurled, void of powder, and dank with dew. His clothes were huddled on with a careless negligence remarkable in a military man, whose real or supposed duties are usually held to include some attention to the toilet; and his looks were haggard and ghastly in a peculiar degree.

'So you have stolen a march upon us this morning, my dear General,' said Lord Woodville; 'or you have not found your bed so much to your mind as I had hoped and you seemed to expect. How did you rest last night?'

'Oh, excellently well—remarkably well—never better in my life!' said General Browne rapidly, and yet with an air of embarrassment which was obvious to his friend. He then hastily swallowed a cup of tea, and, neglecting or refusing whatever else he was offered, seemed to fall into a fit of abstraction.

'You will take the gun to-day, General?' said his friend and host, but had to repeat the question twice ere he received the abrupt answer, 'No, my Lord; I am sorry I cannot have the honour of spending another day with your lordship; my post-horses are ordered, and will be here directly.'

All who were present showed surprise, and Lord Woodville immediately replied, 'Post-horses, my good friend! What can you possibly want with them, when you promised to stay with me quietly for at least a week?'

'I believe,' said the General, obviously much embarrased, 'that I might, in the pleasure of my first meeting with your lordship, have said something about stopping here a few days; but I have since found it altogether impossible.'

'That is very extraordinary,' answered the young nobleman. 'You seemed quite disengaged yesterday, and you cannot have had a summons to-day, for our post has not come up from town, and therefore you cannot have received any letters.'

General Browne, without giving any further explanation, muttered something of indispensable business, and insisted on the absolute necessity of his departure in a manner which silenced all opposition on the part of his host, who saw that his resolution was taken, and forbore all further importunity.

'At least, however,' he said, 'permit me, my dear Browne, since go you will or must, to show you the view from the terrace, which the mist, that is now rising, will soon display.'

He threw open a sash-window and stepped down upon the terrace as he spoke. The General followed him mechanically, but seemed little to attend to what his host was saying, as, looking across an extended and rich prospect, he pointed out the different objects worthy of observation. Thus they moved on till Lord Woodville had attained his purpose of drawing his guest entirely apart from the rest of the company, when, turning round upon him with an air of great solemnity, he addressed him thus:

'Richard Browne, my old and very dear friend, we are now alone. Let me conjure you to answer me upon the word of a friend and the honour of a soldier. How did you in reality rest during the night?'

'Most wretchedly indeed, my lord,' answered the General, in the same tone of solemnity; 'so miserably, that I would not run the risk of such a second night, not only for all the lands belonging to this castle, but for all the country which I see from this elevated point of view.'

'This is most extraordinary,' said the young lord, as if speaking to himself; 'then there must be something in the reports concerning that apartment.' Again turning to the General, he said, 'For God's sake, my dear friend, be candid with me and let me know the disagreeable particulars which have befallen you under a roof where, with consent of the owner, you should have met nothing save comfort.'

The General seemed distressed by this appeal, and paused

a moment before he replied. 'My dear lord,' he at length said, 'what happened to me last night is of a nature so peculiar and so unpleasant, that I could hardly bring myself to detail it even to your lordship, were it not that, independent of my wish to gratify any request of yours, I think that sincerity on my part may lead to some explanation about a circumstance equally painful and mysterious. To others, the communication I am about to make might place me in the light of a weak-minded, superstitious fool, who suffered his own imagination to delude and bewilder him; but you have known me in childhood and youth, and will not suspect me of having adopted in manhood the feelings and frailties from which my early years were free.' Here he paused, and his friend replied:

'Do not doubt my perfect confidence in the truth of your communication, however strange it may be,' replied Lord Woodville; 'I know your firmness of disposition too well to suspect you could be made the object of imposition, and am aware that your honour and your friendship will equally deter you from exaggerating whatever you may have witnessed.'

'Well, then,' said the General, 'I will proceed with my story as well as I can, relying upon your candour, and yet distinctly feeling that I would rather face a battery than recall to my mind the odious recollections of last night.'

He paused a second time, and then perceiving that Lord Woodville remained silent and in an attitude of attention, he commenced, though not without obvious reluctance, the history of his night adventures in the Tapestried Chamber.

'I undressed and went to bed, so soon as your lordship left me yesterday evening; but the wood in the chimney, which nearly fronted my bed, blazed brightly and cheerfully, and, aided by a hundred recollections of my childhood and youth, which had been recalled by the unexpected pleasure of meeting your lordship, prevented me from falling immediately asleep. I ought, however, to say that these reflections were all of a pleasant and agreeable kind, grounded on a sense of having for a time exchanged the labour, fatigues and dangers of my profession for the enjoyments of a peaceful life, and the reunion of those friendly and affectionate ties which I had torn asunder at the rude summons of war.

'While such pleasing reflections were stealing over my mind, and gradually lulling me to slumber, I was suddenly aroused by a sound like that of the rustling of a silken gown and the tapping of a pair of high-heeled shoes, as if a woman were walking in the apartment. Ere I could draw the curtain to see what the matter was, the figure of a little woman passed between the bed and the fire. The back of this form was turned to me, and I could observe, from the shoulders and neck, it was that of an old woman, whose dress was an old-fashioned gown, which, I think, ladies call a sacque—that is, a sort of robe completely loose in the body, but gathered into broad plaits upon the neck and shoulders, which fall down to the ground, and terminate in a species of train.

'I thought the intrusion singular enough, but never harboured for a moment the idea that what I saw was anything more than the mortal form of some old woman about the establishment, who had a fancy to dress like her grandmother, and who, having perhaps, as your lordship mentioned that you were rather straitened for room, been dislodged from her chamber for my accommodation, had forgotten the circumstances and returned by twelve to her old haunt. Under this persuasion I moved myself in bed and coughed a little, to make the intruder sensible of my being in possession of the premises. She turned slowly round, but, gracious Heaven! my lord, what a countenance did she display to me! There was no longer any question what she was, or any thought of her being a living being.

Upon a face which wore the fixed features of a corpse were imprinted the traces of the vilest and most hideous passions which had animated her while she lived. The body of some atrocious criminal seemed to have been given up from the grave, and the soul restored from the penal fire, in order to form, for a space, an union with the ancient accomplice of its guilt. I started up in bed, and sat upright, supporting myself on my palms, as I gazed on this horrible spectre. The hag made, as it seemed, a single and swift stride to the bed where I lay, and squatted herself down upon it, in precisely the same attitude which I had assumed in the extremity of horror, advancing her diabolical countenance within half a yard of mine, with a grin which seemed to intimate the malice and the derision of an incarnate fiend.'

Here General Browne stopped, and wiped from his brow the cold perspiration with which the recollection of his horrible vision had covered it.

'My lord,' he said, 'I am no coward. I have been in all the mortal dangers incidental to my profession, and I may truly boast that no man ever knew Richard Browne dishonour the sword he wears; but in these horrible circumstances, under the eyes, and, as it seemed, almost in the grasp, of an incarnation of an evil spirit, all firmness forsook me, all manhood melted from me like wax in the furnace, and I felt my hair individually bristle. The current of my life-blood ceased to flow, and I sank back in a swoon, as very a victim to panic terror as ever was a village girl or a child of ten years old. How long I lay in this condition I cannot pretend to guess.

'But I was roused by the castle clock striking one, so loud that it seemed as if it were in the very room. It was some time before I dared open my eyes, lest they should again encounter the horrible spectacle. When, however, I summoned courage to look up, she was no longer visible. My first idea was to pull my bell, wake the servants, and remove to a garret or a hay-loft, to be ensured against a second visitation. Nay, I will confess the truth, that my resolution was altered, not by the shame of exposing myself, but by the fear that, as the bell-cord hung by the chimney, I might, in making my way to it, be again crossed by the fiendish hag, who, I figured to myself, might be still lurking about some corner of the apartment.

'I will not pretend to describe what hot and cold fever-fits tormented me for the rest of the night, through broken sleep, weary vigils, and that dubious state which forms the neutral ground between them. An hundred terrible objects appeared to haunt me; but there was the great difference betwixt the vision which I have described and those which followed, that I knew the last to be deceptions of my own fancy and over-excited nerves.

'Day at last appeared, and I rose from my bed ill in health and humiliated in mind. I was ashamed of myself as a man and a soldier, and still more so at feeling my own extreme desire to escape from the haunted apartment, which, however, conquered all other considerations; so that, huddling on my clothes with the most careless haste, I made my escape from your lordship's mansion, to seek in the open air some relief to my nervous system, shaken as it was by this horrible encounter with a visitant, for such I must believe her, from the other world. Your lordship has now heard the cause of my discomposure, and of my sudden desire to leave your hospitable castle. In other places I trust we may often meet; but God protect me from ever spending a second night under that roof!'

Strange as the General's tale was, he spoke with such a deep air of conviction, that it cut short all the usual commentaries which are made on such stories. Lord Woodville never once asked him if he was sure he did not dream of the apparition, or suggested any of the possibilities by which it is fashionable to explain supernatural appearances, as wild vagaries of the fancy or deceptions of the optic nerves. On the contrary, he seemed deeply impressed with the truth and reality of what he had heard; and, after a considerable pause, regretted, with much appearance of sincerity, that his early friend should in his house have suffered so severely.

'I am the more sorry for your pain, my dear Browne,' he continued, 'that it is the unhappy, though most unexpected, result of an experiment of my own. You must know that, for my father and grandfather's time, at least, the apartment which was assigned to you last night had been shut on account of reports that it was disturbed by supernatural sights and noises. When I came, a few weeks since, into possession of the estate, I thought the accommodation which the castle afforded for my friends was not extensive enough to permit the inhabitants of the invisible world to retain possession of a comfortable sleeping-apartment. I therefore caused the Tapestried Chamber, as we call it, to be opened, and, without destroying its air of antiquity, I had such new articles of furniture placed in it as became the modern times. Yet, as the opinion that the room was haunted very strongly prevailed among the domestics, and was also known in the neighbourhood and to many of my friends, I feared some prejudice might be entertained by the first occupant of the Tapestried Chamber, which might tend to revive the evil report which it had laboured under, and so disappoint my purpose of rendering it a useful part of the house. I must confess, my dear Browne, that your arrival yesterday, agreeable to me for a thousand reasons besides, seemed the most favourable opportunity of removing the unpleasant rumours which attached to the room, since your courage was indubitable, and your mind free of any pre-occupation on the subject. I could not, therefore, have chosen a more fitting subject for my experiment.'

'Upon my life,' said General Browne, somewhat hastily, 'I am infinitely obliged to your lordship—very particulary indebted indeed. I am likely to remember for some time the consequences of the experiment, as your lordship is pleased to call it.'

'Nay, now you are unjust, my dear friend,' said Lord Woodville. 'You have only to reflect for a single moment, in order to be convinced that I could not augur the possibility of the pain to which you have been so unhappily exposed. I was yesterday morning a complete sceptic on the subject of supernatural appearances. Nay, I am sure that, had I told you what was said about that room, those very reports would have induced you, by your own choice, to select it for your accommodation. It was my misfortune, perhaps my error, but really cannot be termed my fault, that you have been afflicted so strangely.'

'Strangely indeed!' said the General, resuming his good temper; 'and I acknowledge that I have no right to be offended with your lordship for treating me like what I used to think myself, a man of some firmness and courage. But I see my post-horses are arrived, and I must not detain your lordship from your amusement.'

'Nay, my old friend,' said Lord Woodville, 'since you cannot stay with us another day, which, indeed, I can no longer urge, give me at least half an hour more. You used to love pictures, and I have a gallery of portraits, some of them by Vandyke, representing ancestry to whom this property and castle formerly belonged. I think that several of them will strike you as possessing merit.'

General Browne accepted the invitation, though somewhat unwillingly. It was evident he was not to breathe freely or at ease till he left Woodville Castle far behind him. He could not refuse his friend's invitation, however; and the less so, that he was a little ashamed of the peevishness which he had displayed towards his well-meaning entertainer.

The General, therefore, followed Lord Woodville through several rooms, into a long gallery hung with pictures, which the latter pointed out to his guest, telling the names, and giving some account of the personages whose portraits presented themselves in progression. General Browne was but little interested in the details which these accounts conveyed to him. They were, indeed, of the kind which are usually found in an old family gallery. Here was a cavalier who had ruined the estate in the royal cause; there was a fine lady who had reinstated it by contracting a match with a wealthy Roundhead. There hung a gallant who had been in danger for corresponding with the exiled court at St. Germain's; here one who had taken arms for William at the Revolution; and there a third that had thrown his weight alternately into the scale of Whig and Tory.

While Lord Woodville was cramming these words into his guest's hear, 'against the stomach of his sense,' they gained the middle of the gallery, when he beheld General Browne suddenly start, and assume an attitude of the utmost surprise, not unmixed with fear, as his eyes were caught and suddenly riveted by a portrait of an old lady in a sacque, the fashionable dress of the end of the 17th century.

'There she is!' he exclaimed—'there she is, in form and features, though inferior in demoniac expression to the accursed hag who visited me last night.'

'If that be the case,' said the young nobleman, 'there can remain no longer any doubt of the horrible reality of your apparition. That is the picture of a wretched ancestress of mine, of whose crimes a black and fearful catalogue is recorded in a family history in my charter-chest. The recital of them would be too horrible; it is enough to say, that in yon fatal apartment incest and unnatural murder were committed. I will restore it to the solitude to which the better judgement of those who preceded me had consigned it; and never shall any one, so long as I can prevent it, be exposed to a repetition of the supernatural horrors which could shake such courage as yours.'

Thus, the friends, who had met with such glee, parted in a very different mood—Lord Woodville to command the Tapestried Chamber to be unmantled and the door built up; and General Browne to seek in some less beautiful country, and with some less dignified friend, forgetfulness of the painful night which he had passed in Woodville Castle.

from *The Keepsake* 1828

MY AUNT MARGARET'S MIRROR

MY AUNT MARGARET'S MIRROR

There are times
When Fancy plays her gambols, in despite
Even of our watchful senses, when in sooth
Substance seems shadow, shadow substance seems,
When the broad, palpable, and mark'd partition,
'Twixt that which is and is not, seems dissolved,
As if the mental eye gain'd power to gaze
Beyond the limits of the existing world.
Such hours of shadowy dreams I better love
Than all the gross realities of life.—Anonymous

M Y Aunt Margaret was one of that respected sisterhood, upon whom devolve all the trouble and solicitude incidental to the possession of children, excepting only that which attends their entrance into the world. We were a large family, of very different dispositions and constitutions. Some were dull and peevish—they were sent to Aunt Margaret to be amused; some were rude, romping, and boisterous—they were sent to Aunt Margaret to be kept quiet, or rather that their noise might be removed out of hearing: those who were indisposed were sent with the prospect of being nursed—those who were stubborn, with the hope of their being subdued by the kindness of Aunt Margaret's discipline; in short, she had all the various duties of a mother, without the credit and dignity of the maternal character. The busy scene of her various cares is now over—of the invalids and the robust, the kind and the rough, the peevish and pleased children, who thronged her little parlour from morning to night, not one now remains alive but myself; who, afflicted by early infirmity, was one of the most delicate of her nurslings, yet nevertheless, have out-lived them all.

It is still my custom, and shall be so while I have the use of my limbs, to visit my respected relation at least three times a week. Her abode is about half a mile from the suburbs of the town in which I reside; and is accessible, not only by the high road from which it stands at some distance but by means of a greensward footpath, leading through some pretty meadows. I have so little left to torment me in life, that it is one of my greatest vexations to know that several of these sequestered fields have been devoted as sites for building. In that which is nearest the town, wheelbarrows have been at work for several weeks in such numbers that, I verily believe, its whole surface, to the depth of at least eighteen inches, was mounted in these monotrochs at the same moment, and in the act of being transported from one place to another. Huge triangular piles of planks are also reared in different parts of the devoted messuage; and a little group of trees, that still grace the eastern end which rises in a gentle ascent, have just received warning to quit expressed by a daub of white paint, and are to give place to a curious grove of chimneys.

It would, perhaps, hurt others in my situation to reflect that this little range of pasturage once belonged to my father (whose family was of some consideration in the world) and was sold by patches to remedy distresses in which he involved himself in an attempt by commercial adventure to redeem his diminished fortune. While the building scheme was in full operation, this circumstance was often pointed out to me by the class of friends who are anxious that no part of your misfortunes should escape your observation. 'Such pasture-ground!—lying at the very town's end—in turnips and potatoes, the parks would bring £20 per acre, and if leased for building—Oh, it was a gold mine!—And all sold for an old song out of the ancient possessor's hands!' My comforters cannot bring me to repine much on this subject. If I could be allowed to look back on the past without interruption, I could willingly give up the enjoyment of present income, and the hope of future profit, to those who have purchased what my father sold. I regret the alteration of the ground only because it destroys associations, and I would more willingly (I think) see the Earl's Closes in the hands of strangers, retaining their sylvan appearance, than know them for my own, if torn up by agriculture, or covered with buildings. Mine are the sensations of poor Logan:

> *The horrid plough has rased the green*
> *Where yet a child I stray'd;*
> *The axe has fell'd the hawthorn screen,*
> *The schoolboy's summer shade.*

I hope, however, the threatened devastation will not be consummated in my day. Although the adventurous spirit of times short while since passed gave rise to the undertaking, I have been encouraged to think that the subsequent changes have so far damped the spirit of speculation, that the rest of the woodland footpath leading to Aunt Margaret's retreat will be left undisturbed for her time and mine. I am interested in this, for every step of the way, after I have passed through the green already mentioned, has for me something of early remembrance:—There is the stile at which I can recollect a cross child's-maid upbraiding me with my infirmity, as she lifted me coarsely and carelessly over the flinty steps, which my brothers traversed with shout and bound. I remember the suppressed bitterness of the moment, and, conscious of my own inferiority, the feeling of envy with which I regarded the easy movements and elastic steps of my more happily formed brethren. Alas! these goodly barks have all perished on life's wide ocean, and only that which seemed so little seaworthy, as the naval

phrase goes, has reached the port when the tempest is over.
Then there is the pool, where, manoeuvring our little navy,
constructed out of the broad water flags, my elder brother
fell in, was scarce saved from the watery element to die
under Nelson's banner. There is the hazel copse also, in
which my brother Henry used to gather nuts, thinking little
that he was to die in an Indian jungle in quest of rupees.

There is so much more of remembrance about the little
walk that—as I stop, rest on my crutch-headed cane, and
look round with that species of comparison between the
thing I was and that which I now am—it almost induces me
to doubt my own identity; until I find myself in face of the
honeysuckle porch of Aunt Margaret's dwelling, with its
irregularity of front, and its odd projecting latticed
windows; where the workmen seem to have made a study
that no one of them should resemble another, in form, size,
or in the old-fashioned stone entablature and labels which
adorn them. This tenement, once the manor-house of Earl's
Closes, we still retain a slight hold upon; for, in some family
arrangements, it had been settled upon Aunt Margaret
during the term of her life. Upon this frail tenure depends,
in a great measure, the last shadow of the family of
Bothwell of Earl's Closes, and their last slight connexion
with their paternal inheritance. The only representative will
then be an infirm old man, moving not unwillingly to the
grave, which has devoured all that were dear to his affections.

When I have indulged such thoughts for a minute or two,
I enter the mansion which is said to have been the gatehouse
only of the original building, and find one being on whom
time seems to have made little impression; for the Aunt
Margaret of to-day bears the same proportional age to the
Aunt Margaret of my early youth, that the boy of ten years
old does to the man of (by'r Lady!) some fifty-six years. The
old lady's invariable costume has doubtless some share in

confirming one in the opinion that time has stood still with Aunt Margaret.

The brown or chocolate-coloured silk gown, with ruffles of the same stuff at the elbow, within which are others of Mechlin lace—the black silk gloves, or mitts, the white hair combed back upon a roll, and the cap of spotless cambric, which closes around the venerable countenance, as they were not the costume of 1780, so neither were they that of 1826; they are altogether a style peculiar to the individual Aunt Margaret. There she still sits, as she sat thirty years since, with her wheel or the stocking, which she works by the fire in winter and by the window in summer; or, perhaps, venturing as far as the porch in an unusually fine summer evening. Her frame, like some well-constructed piece of mechanics, still performs the operations for which it had seemed destined; going its round with an activity which is gradually diminished, yet indicating no probability that it will soon come to a period.

The solicitude and affection which had made Aunt Margaret the willing slave to the inflictions of a whole nursery, have now for their object the health and comfort of one old and infirm man, the last remaining relative of her family, and the only one who can still find interest in the traditional stores which she hoards, as some miser hides the gold which he desires that no one should enjoy after his death.

My conversation with Aunt Margaret generally relates little either to the present or to the future: for the passing day we possess as much as we require, and we neither of us wish for more; and for that which is to follow we have on this side of the grave neither hopes, nor fears, nor anxiety. We therefore naturally look back to the past; and forget the present fallen fortunes and declined importance of our family, in recalling the hours when it was wealthy and prosperous.

With this slight introduction, the reader will know as much of Aunt Margaret and her nephew as is necessary to comprehend the following conversation and narrative.

Last week, when, late in a summer evening, I went to call on the old lady to whom my reader is now introduced, I was received by her with all her usual affection and benignity; while, at the same time, she seemed abstracted and disposed to silence. I asked her the reason. 'They have been clearing out the old chapel,' she said; 'John Clayhudgeons having, it seems, discovered that the stuff within—being, I suppose, the remains of our ancestors—was excellent for top-dressing the meadows.'

Here I started up with more alacrity than I have displayed for some years; but sat down while my aunt added, laying her hand upon my sleeve, 'The chapel has been long considered as common ground, my dear, and used for a penfold, and what objection can we have to the man for employing what is his own, to his own profit? Besides, I did speak to him, and he very readily and civilly promised that, if he found bones or monuments, they should be carefully respected and reinstated; and what more could I ask? So, the first stone they found bore the name of Margaret Bothwell, 1585, and I have caused it to be laid carefully aside, as I think it betokens death; and having served my namesake two hundred years, it has just been cast up in time to do me the same good turn. My house has been long put in order, as far as the small earthly concerns require it, but who shall say that their account with Heaven is sufficiently revised?'

'After what you have said, aunt,' I replied, 'perhaps I ought to take my hat and go away, and so I should, but that there is on this occasion a little alloy mingled with our devotion. To think of death at all times is a duty—to suppose it nearer, from the finding of an old gravestone, is superstition; and you, with your strong useful common sense which was so long the prop of a fallen family, are the last person whom I should have suspected of such weakness.'

'Neither would I have deserved your suspicions, kinsman,' answered Aunt Margaret, 'if we were speaking of any incident occuring in the actual business of human life. But for all this I have a sense of superstition about me, which I do not wish to part with. It is a feeling which separates me from this age, and links me with that to which I am hastening; and even when it seems, as now, to lead me to the brink of the grave, and bids me gaze on it, I do not love that it should be dispelled. It soothes my imagination, without influencing my reason or conduct.'

'I profess, my good lady,' replied I, 'that had any one but you made such a declaration, I should have thought it as capricious as that of the clergyman who, without vindicating his false reading, preferred, from habit's sake, his old Mumpsimus to the modern Sumpsimus.'

'Well,' answered my aunt, 'I must explain my inconsistency in this particular, by comparing it to another. I am, as you know, a piece of that old-fashioned thing called a Jacobite, but I am so in sentiment and feeling only; for a more loyal subject never joined in prayers for the health and wealth of George the Fourth, whom God long preserve! But I dare say that kind-hearted sovereign would not deem that an old woman did him much injury if she leaned back in her armchair, just in such a twilight as this, and thought of the high-mettled men whose sense of duty called to arms against his grandfather; and how, in a cause which they deemed that of their rightful prince and country,

> *The fought till their hands to the broadsword were glued*
> *They fought against fortune with hearts unsubdued.*

Do not come at such a moment, when my head is full of plaids, pibrochs, and claymores, and ask my reason to admit what, I am afraid, it cannot deny—I mean, that the public advantage peremptorily demanded that these things should cease to exist. I cannot, indeed, refuse to allow the justice of your reasoning; but yet, being convinced against my will, you will gain little by your motion. You might as well read to an infatuated lover the catalogue of his mistress's imperfections; for, when he has been compelled to listen to the summary, you will only get for answer, that " he lo'es her a' the better." '

I was not sorry to have changed the gloomy train of Aunt Margaret's thoughts, and replied in the same tone, 'Well, I can't help being persuaded that our good king is the more sure of Mrs. Bothwell's loyal affection, that he has the Stuart right of birth, as well as the Act of Succession in his favour.'

'Perhaps my attachment, were its source of consequence, might be found warmer for the union of the rights you mention,' said Aunt Margaret; 'but upon my word, it would be as sincere if the king's right were founded only on the will of the nation, as declared at the Revolution. I am none of your *jure divino* folk,'

'And a Jacobite notwithstanding.'

'And a Jacobite notwithstanding; or rather, I will give you leave to call me one of the party which, in Queen Anne's time, were called *Whimsicals;* because they were sometimes operated upon by feelings, sometimes by principle. After all, it is very hard that you will not allow an old woman to be as inconsistent in her political sentiments as mankind in general show themselves in all the various courses of life; since you cannot point out one of them, in which the passions and prejudices of those who pursue it are not perpetually carrying us away from the path which our reason points out.'

'True, aunt; but you are a wilful wanderer, who should be forced back into the right path.'

'Spare me, I entreat you,' replied Aunt Margaret. 'You

remember the Gaelic song, though I dare say I mispronounce the words—

Hatil mohatil na dowski mi
I am asleep, do not waken me.

I tell you, kinsman, that the sort of waking dreams which my imagination spins out, in what your favourite Wordsworth calls "moods of my own mind", are worth all the rest of my more active days. Then, instead of looking forwards as I did in youth, and forming for myself fairy palaces upon the verge of the grave, I turn my eyes backward upon the days and manners of my better time; and the sad, yet soothing recollections come so close and interesting, that I almost think it sacrilege to be wiser, or more rational, or less prejudiced, than those to whom I looked up in my younger years.'

'I think I now understand what you mean,' I answered, 'and can comprehend why you should occasionally prefer the twilight of illusion to the steady light of reason.'

'Where there is no task,' she rejoined, 'to be performed, we may sit in the dark if we like it—if we go to work, we must ring for candles.'

'And amidst such shadowy and doubtful light,' continued I, 'imagination frames her enchanted and enchanting visions, and sometimes passes them upon the senses for reality.'

'Yes,' said Aunt Margaret, who is a well-read woman, 'to those who resemble the translator of Tasso,

Prevailing poet, whose undoubting mind
Believed the magic wonders which he sung.

It is not required for this purpose, that you should be sensible of the painful horrors which an actual belief in such prodigies inflicts—such a belief, now-a-days, belongs only to fools and children. It is not necessary that your ears should tingle, and your complexion change, like that of Theodore, at the approach of the spectral huntsman. All that is indispensable for the enjoyment of the milder feeling of supernatural awe is that you should be susceptible of the slight shuddering which creeps over you when you hear a tale of terror—that well-vouched tale which the narrator, having first expressed his general disbelief of all such legendary lore, selects and produces, as having something in it which he has been always obliged to give up as inexplicable. Another symptom is, a momentary hesitation to look round you when the interest of the narrative is at the highest; and the third, a desire to avoid looking into a mirror, when you are alone in your chamber for the evening. I mean such are signs which indicate the crisis, when a female imagination is in due temperature to enjoy a ghost story. I do not pretend to describe those which express the same disposition in a gentleman.'

'This last symptom, dear aunt, of shunning the mirror, seems likely to be a rare occurrence amongst the fair sex.'

'You are a novice in toilet fashions, my dear kinsman. All women consult the looking-glass with anxiety before they go into company; but when they return home, the mirror has not the same charm. The die has been cast—the party has been successful in the impression which she desired to make. But, without going deeper into the mysteries of the dressing-table, I will tell you that I myself, like many other honest folk, do not like to see the blank black front of a large mirror in a room dimly lighted, and where the reflection of the candle seems rather to lose itself in the deep obscurity of the glass, than to be reflected back again into the apartment. That space of inky darkness seems to be a field for fancy to play her revels in. She may call up other features to meet us, instead of the reflection of our own; or, as in the spells of Hallowe'en, which we learned in childhood, some unknown form may be seen peeping over our shoulder. In short, when I am in a ghost-seeing humour, I make my handmaiden draw the green curtains over the mirror before I go into the room, so that she may have the first shock of the apparition, if there be any to be seen. But, to tell you the truth, this dislike to look into a mirror in particular times and places, has, I believe, its original foundation in a story which came to me by tradition from my grandmother, who was a party concerned in the scene of which I will now tell you.'

THE MIRROR

Chapter 1

You are fond (said my aunt of sketches of the society which has passed away. I wish I could describe to you Sir Philip Forester, the "chartered libertine" of Scottish good company, about the end of the last century. I never saw him indeed; but my mother's traditions were full of his wit, gallantry, and dissipation. This gay knight flourished about the end of the seventeenth and beginning of the eighteenth century. He was the Sir Charles Easy and the Lovelace of his day and country: renowned for the number of duels he had fought, and the successful intrigues which he had carried on. The supremacy which he had attained in the fashionable world was absolute; and when we combine it with one or two anecdotes, for which, "if laws were made for every degree," he ought certainly to have been hanged, the popularity of such a person really serves to show, either that the present times are much more decent, if not more virtuous, than they formerly were; or that high breeding then was of more difficult attainment than that which is now so called; and, consequently, entitled the successful professor to a proportionable degree of plenary indulgences and privileges. No beau of this day could have borne out so ugly a story as that of Pretty Peggy Grindstone, the miller's daughter at Sillermills—it had wellnigh made work for the Lord Advocate. But it hurt Sir Philip Forester no more than the hail hurts the hearthstone. He was as well received in society as ever, and dined with the Duke of A—— the day the poor girl was buried. She died of heartbreak. But that has nothing to do with my story.

Now, you must listen to a single word upon kith, kin, and ally; I promise you I will not be prolix. But it is necessary to the authenticity of my legend that you should know that Sir Philip Forester, with his handsome person, elegant accomplishments, and fashionable manners, married the younger Miss Falconer of King's Copland. The elder sister of this lady had previously become the wife of my grandfather, Sir Geoffrey Bothwell, and brought into our family a good fortune. Miss Jemima, or Miss Jemmie Falconer, as she was usually called, had also about ten thousand pounds sterling—then thought a very handsome portion indeed.

The two sisters were extremely different, though each had their admirers while they remained single. Lady Bothwell had some touch of the old King's-Copland blood about her. She was bold, though not to the degree of audacity; ambitious, and desirous to raise her house and family; and was, as has been said, a considerable spur to my grandfather, who was otherwise an indolent man; but whom, unless he has been slandered, his lady's influence involved in some political matters which had been more wisely let alone. She was a woman of high principle, however, and musculine good sense, as some of her letters testify, which are still in my wainscot cabinet.

Jemmie Falconer was the reverse of her sister in every

respect. Her understanding did not reach above the ordinary pitch, if, indeed, she could be said to have attained it. Her beauty, while it lasted, consisted, in a great measure, of delicacy of complexion and regularity of features, without any peculiar force of expression. Even these charms faded under the sufferings attendant on an ill-sorted match. She was passionately attached to her husband, by whom she was treated with a callous, yet polite indifference, which, to one whose heart was as tender as her judgement was weak, was more painful perhaps than absolute ill-usage. Sir Philip was a voluptuary, that is, a completely selfish egotist, whose disposition and character resembled the rapier he wore, polished, keen, and brilliant, but inflexible and unpitying. As he observed carefully all the usual forms towards his lady, he had the art to deprive her even of the compassion of the world; and useless and unavailing as that may be while actually possessed by the sufferer, it is, to a mind like lady Forester's, most painful to know she has it not.

The tattle of society did its best to place the peccant husband above the suffering wife. Some called her a poor spiritless thing, and declared that, with a little of her sister's spirit, she might have brought to reason any Sir Philip whatsoever, were it the termagant Falconbridge himself. But the greater part of their acquaintance affected candour, and saw faults on both sides; though, in fact, there only existed the oppressor and the oppressed. The tone of such critics was—'To be sure, no one will justify Sir Philip Forester, but then we all know Sir Philip, and Jemmie Falconer might have known what she had to expect from the beginning.— What made her set her cap at Sir Philip?—He would never have looked at her if she had not thrown herself at his head, with her poor ten thousand pounds. I am sure, if it is money he wanted, she spoiled his market. I know where Sir Philip could have done much better.—And then, if she *would* have the man, could not she try to make him more comfortable at home, and have his friends oftener, and not plague him with the squalling children, and take care all was handsome and in good style about the house? I declare I think Sir Philip would have made a very domestic man, with a woman who knew how to manage him.'

Now these fair critics, in raising their profound edifice of domestic felicity, did not recollect that the corner-stone was wanting; and that to receive good company with good cheer, the means of the banquet ought to have been furnished by Sir Philip; whose income (dilapidated as it was) was not equal to the display of hospitality required, and, at the same time, to the supply of the good knight's *menus plaisirs*. So, in spite of all that was so sagely suggested by female friends, Sir Philip carried his good-humour everywhere abroad, and left at home a solitary mansion and a pining spouse.

At length, inconvenienced in his money affairs, and tired even of the short time which he spent in his own dull house, Sir Philip Forester determined to take a trip to the Continent, in the capacity of a volunteer. It was then common for men of fashion to do so; and our knight perhaps was of opinion that a touch of the military character, just enough to exalt, but not render pedantic, his qualities as a beau *garçon,* was necessary to maintain possession of the elevated situation which he held in the ranks of fashion.

Sir Philip's resolution threw his wife into agonies of terror, by which the worthy baronet was so much annoyed that, contrary to his wont, he took some trouble to soothe her apprehensions; and once more brought her to shed tears, in which sorrow was not altogether unmingled with pleasure. Lady Bothwell asked, as a favour, Sir Philip's permission to receive her sister and her family into her own house during his absence on the Continent. Sir Philip readily assented to a proposition which saved expense, silenced the foolish people who might have talked of a deserted wife and family, and gratified Lady Bothwell, for whom he felt some respect, as for one who often spoke to him, always with freedom, and sometimes with severity, without being deterred either by his raillery, or the prestige of his reputation.

A day or two before Sir Philip's departure, Lady Bothwell took the liberty of asking him, in her sister's presence, the direct question, which his timid wife had often desired, but never ventured, to put to him.

'Pray, Sir Philip, what route do you take when you reach the Continent?'

'I go from Leith to Helvoet by a packet with advices.'

'That I comprehend perfectly,' said Lady Bothwell dryly; 'but you do not mean to remain long at Helvoet, I presume, and I should like to know what is your next object?'

'You ask me, my dear lady,' answered Sir Philip, 'a question which I have not dared to ask myself. The answer depends on the fate of war. I shall, of course, go to head-quarters, wherever they may happen to be for the time; deliver my letters of introduction; learn as much of the noble art of war as may suffice a poor interloping amateur; and then take a glance at the sort of thing of which we read so much in the *Gazette*.'

'And I trust, Sir Philip,' said Lady Bothwell, 'that you will remember that you are a husband and a father; and that though you think fit to indulge this military fancy, you will not let it hurry you into dangers which it is certainly un-necessary for any save professional persons to encounter?''

'Lady Bothwell does me too much honour,' replied the adventurous knight, 'in regarding such a circumstance with the slightest interest. But to soothe your flattering anxiety, I trust your ladyship will recollect that I cannot expose to hazard the venerable and paternal character which you so obligingly recommend to my protection, without putting in some peril an honest fellow called Philip Forester, with whom I have kept company for thirty years, and with whom, though some folk consider him a coxcomb, I have not the least desire to part.'

'Well, Sir Philip, you are the best judge of your own affairs; I have little right to interfere – you are not my husband.'

'God forbid!' – said Sir Philip; instantly adding, however, 'God forbid that I should deprive my friend Sir Geoffrey of so inestimable a treasure."

'But you are my sister's husband,' replied the lady; 'and I suppose you are aware of her present distress of mind . . . .'

'If hearing of nothing else from morning to night can make me aware of it,' said Sir Philip, 'I should know something of the matter.'

'I do not pretend to reply to your wit, Sir Philip,' answered Lady Bothwell; 'but you must be sensible that all this distress is on account of apprehensions for your personal safety.'

'In that case, I am surprised that Lady Bothwell, at least, should give herself so much trouble upon so insignificant a subject.'

'My sister's interest may account for my being anxious to learn something of Sir Philip Forester's motions; about which otherwise, I know, he would not wish me to concern myself. I have a brother's safety, too, to be anxious for.'

'You mean Major Falconer, your brother by the mother's side: – What can he possibly have to do with our present agreeable conversation?'

'You have had words together, Sir Philip,' said Lady Bothwell.

'Naturally; we are connexions,' replied Sir Philip, 'and as such have always had the usual intercourse.'

'That is an evasion of the subject,' answered the lady. 'By words, I mean angry words, on the subject of your usage of your wife.'

'If,' replied Sir Philip Forester, 'you suppose Major Falconer simple enough to intrude his advice upon me, Lady Bothwell, in my domestic matters, you are indeed warranted in believing that I might possibly be so far displeased with the interference as to request him to reserve his advice till it was asked.'

'And, being on these terms, you are going to join the very army in which my brother Falconer is now serving?'

'No man knows the path of honour better than Major Falconer,' said Sir Philip. 'An aspirant after fame, like me, cannot choose a better guide than his footsteps.'

Lady Bothwell rose and went to the window, the tears gushing from her eyes.

'And this heartless raillery,' she said, 'is all the consideration that is to be given to our apprehensions of a quarrel which may bring on the most terrible consequences? Good God! of what can men's hearts be made, who can thus dally with the agony of others?'

Sir Philip Forester was moved; he laid aside the mocking tone in which he had hitherto spoken.

'Dear Lady Bothwell,' he said, taking her reluctant hand, 'we are both wrong: – you are too deeply serious; I, perhaps, too little so. The dispute I had with Major Falconer was of no earthly consequence. Had anything occurred betwixt us that ought to have been settled *par voie du fait,* as we say in France, neither of us are persons that are likely to postpone such a meeting. Permit me to say that were it generally known that you or my Lady Forester are apprehensive of such a catastrophe, it might be the very means of bringing about what would not otherwise be likely to happen. I know your good sense, Lady Bothwell, and that you will understand me when I say that really my affairs require my absence for some months; – Jemima cannot understand; it is a perpetual recurrence of questions, why can you not do this, or that, or the third thing; and when you have proved to her that her expedients are totally ineffectual, you have just to begin the whole round again. Now, do you tell her, dear Lady Bothwell, that *you* are satisfied. She is, you must confess, one of those persons with whom authority goes further thàn reasoning. Do but repose a little confidence in me, and you shall see how amply I will repay it.'

Lady Bothwell shook her head, as one but half satisfied. 'How difficult it is to extend confidence, when the basis on which it ought to rest has been so much shaken! But I will do my best to make Jemima easy; and further, I can only say that for keeping your present purpose, I hold you responsible both to God and man."

'Do not fear that I will deceive you,' said Sir Philip; 'the safest conveyance to me will be through the general post-office, Helvoetsluys, where I will take care to leave orders for forwarding my letters. As for Falconer, our only encounter will be over a bottle of Burgundy! so make yourself perfectly easy on his score.'

Lady Bothwell could *not* make herself easy; yet she was sensible that her sister hurt her own cause by *taking on,* as the maid-servants call it, too vehemently; and by showing before every stranger, by manner and sometimes by words also, a dissatisfaction with her husband's journey, that was sure to come to his ears and equally certain to displease him. But there was no help for this domestic dissension, which ended only with the day of separation.

I am sorry I cannot tell, with precision, the year in which Sir Philip Forester went over to Flanders; but it was one of those in which the campaign opened with extraordinary fury; and many bloody, though indecisive, skirmishes were fought between the French on the one side, and the Allies on the other. In all our modern improvements, there are none, perhaps, greater than in the accuracy and speed with which intelligence is transmitted from any scene of action to those in this country whom it may concern. During Marlborough's campaigns, the sufferings of the many who had relations in, or along with, the army, were greatly augmented by the suspense in which they were detained for weeks, after they had heard of bloody battles in which, in all probability, those for whom their bosoms throbbed with anxiety had been personally engaged. Amongst those who were most agonized by this state of uncertainty, was the – I had almost said deserted – wife of the gay Sir Philip Forester. A single letter had informed her of his arrival on the Continent – no others were received. One notice occurred in the newspapers, in which Volunteer Sir Philip Forester was mentioned as having been entrusted with a dangerous reconnoissance, which he had executed with the greatest courage, dexterity, and intelligence, and received the thanks of the commanding officer. The sense of his having acquired distinction brought a momentary glow into the lady's pale cheek; but it was instantly lost in ashen whiteness at the recollection of his danger. After this, they had no news whatever, neither from Sir Philip, nor even from their brother Falconer. The case of Lady Forester was not indeed different from that of hundreds in the same situation; but a feeble mind is necessarily an irritable one, and the suspense which some bear with constitutional indifference or philosophical resignation, and some with a disposition to believe and hope the best, was intolerable to Lady Forester, at once solitary and sensitive, low-spirited, and devoid of strength of mind, whether natural or acquired.

Chapter 2

As she received no further news of Sir Philip, whether directly or indirectly, his unfortunate lady began now to feel a sort of consolation, even in those careless habits which had so often given her pain. 'He is so thoughtless,' she repeated a hundred times a day to her sister, 'he never writes when things are going on smoothly; it is his way: had anything happened he would have informed us.'

Lady Bothwell listened to her sister without attempting to console her. Probably she might be of opinion that even the worst intelligence which could be received from Flanders might not be without some touch of consolation; and that the Dowager Lady Forester, if so she was doomed to be called, might have a source of happiness unknown to the wife of the gayest and finest gentleman in Scotland. This conviction became stronger as they learned from inquiries made at headquarters, that Sir Philip was no longer with the army; though whether he had been taken or slain in some of those skirmishes which were perpetually occurring, and in which he loved to distinguish himself, or whether he had, for some unknown reason or capricious change of mind, voluntarily left the service, none of his countrymen in the camp of the Allies could form even a conjecture. Meantime his creditors at home became clamorous, entered into possession of his property, and threatened his person, should he be rash enough to return to Scotland. These additional disadvantages aggravated Lady Bothwell's displeasure against the fugitive husband; while her sister saw nothing in any of them, save what tended to increase her grief for the absence of him whom her imagination now represented – as it had before marriage – gallant, gay, and affectionate.

About this period there appeared in Edinburgh a man of singular appearance and pretensions. He was commonly called the Paduan doctor, from having received his education at that famous university. He was supposed to possess some rare receipts in medicine, with which, it was affirmed, he had wrought remarkable cures. But though, on the one hand, the physicians of Edinburgh termed him an empiric, there were many persons, and among them some of the clergy, who, while they admitted the truth of the cures and the force of his remedies, alleged that Doctor Baptista Damiotti made use of charms and unlawful arts in order to obtain success in his practice. The resorting to him was even solemnly preached against, as a seeking of health from idols, and a trusting to the help which was to come from Egypt. But the protection which the Paduan doctor received from some friends of interest and consequence, enabled him to set these imputations at defiance, and to assume, even in the city of Edinburgh, famed as it was for abhorrence of witches and necromancers, the dangerous character of an expounder of futurity. It was at length rumoured, that for a certain gratification, which, of course, was not an inconsiderable one, Doctor Baptista Damiotti could tell the fate of the absent, and even show his visitors the personal form of their absent friends, and the action in which they were engaged at the moment. This rumour came to the ears of Lady Forester, who had reached that pitch of mental agony in which the sufferer will do anything, or endure anything, that suspense may be converted into certainty.

Gentle and timid in most cases, her state of mind made her equally obstinate and reckless, and it was with no small surprise and alarm that her sister, Lady Bothwell, heard her express a resolution to visit this man of art, and learn from him the fate of her husband. Lady Bothwell remonstrated on the improbability that such pretensions as those of this foreigner could be founded in anything but imposture.

'I care not,' said the deserted wife, 'what degree of ridicule I may incur; if there be any one chance out of a hundred that I may obtain some certainty of my husband's fate, I would not miss that chance for whatever else the world can offer me.'

Lady Bothwell next urged the unlawfulness of resorting to such sources of forbidden knowledge.

'Sister,' replied the sufferer, 'he who is dying of thirst cannot refrain from drinking even poisoned water. She who suffers under suspense must seek information, even were the powers which offer it unhallowed and infernal. I go to learn my fate alone; and this evening will I know it: the sun that rises tomorrow shall find me, if not more happy, at least more resigned.'

'Sister,' said Lady Bothwell, 'if you are determined upon this wild step, you shall not go alone. If this man be an impostor, you may be too much agitated by your feelings to detect his villainy. If, which I cannot believe, there be any truth in what he pretends, you shall not be exposed alone to a communication of so extraordinary a nature. I will go with you, if indeed you determine to go. But yet reconsider your project and renounce inquiries which cannot be prosecuted without guilt, and perhaps without danger.'

Lady Forester threw herself into her sister's arms, and, clasping her to her bosom, thanked her a hundred times for the offer of her company; while she declined with a melancholy gesture the friendly advice with which it was accompanied.

When the hour of twilight arrived, – which was the period when the Paduan doctor was understood to receive the visits of those who came to consult with him, – the two ladies left their apartments in the Canongate of Edinburgh, having their dress arranged like that of women of an inferior description, and their plaids disposed around their faces as they were worn by the same class; for, in those days of aristocracy, the quality of the wearer was generally indicated by the manner in which her plaid was disposed, as well as by the fineness of its texture. It was Lady Bothwell who had suggested this species of disguise, partly to avoid observation as they should go to the conjurer's house, and partly in order to make trial of his penetration, by appearing before him in a feigned character. Lady Forester's servant, of tried fidelity, had been employed by her to propitiate the doctor by a suitable fee, and a story intimating that a soldier's wife desired to know the fate of her husband; a subject upon which, in all probability, the sage was very frequently consulted.

To the last moment, when the palace clock struck eight, Lady Bothwell earnestly watched her sister, in hopes that she might retreat from her rash undertaking; but as mildness, and even timidity, is capable at times of vehement and fixed purposes, she found Lady Forester resolutely unmoved and determined when the moment of departure arrived. Ill satisfied with the expedition, but determined not to leave her sister at such a crisis, Lady Bothwell accompanied Lady Forester through more than one obscure street and lane, the servant walking before, and acting as their guide. At length he suddenly turned into a narrow court, and knocked at an arched door, which seemed to belong to a building of some antiquity. It opened, though no one appeared to act as porter; and the servant, stepping aside from the entrance, motioned the ladies to enter. They had no sooner done so, than it shut, and excluded their guide. The two ladies found themselves in a small vestibule, illuminated by a dim lamp, and having, when the door was closed, no communication with the external light or air. The door of an inner apartment, partly open, was at the further side of the vestibule.

'We must not hesitate now, Jemima,' said Lady Bothwell, and walked forwards into the inner room, where, surrounded by books, maps, philosophical utensils, and other implements of peculiar shape and appearance, they found the man of art.

There was nothing very peculiar in the Italian's appearance. He had the dark complexion and marked feature of his country, seemed about fifty years old, and was handsomely, but plainly dressed in a full suit of black clothes, which was then the universal costume of the medical profession. Large wax-lights, in silver sconces, illuminated the apartment, which was reasonably furnished. He rose as the ladies entered; and, notwithstanding the inferiority of their dress, received them with the marked respect due to their quality, and which foreigners are usually punctilious in rendering to those to whom such honours are due.

Lady Bothwell endeavoured to maintain her proposed incognito; and, as the doctor ushered them to the upper end of the room, made a motion declining his courtesy, as unfitted for their condition. 'We are poor people, sir,' she said; 'only my sister's distress has brought us to consult your worship whether. . . .'

He smiled as he interrupted her – 'I am aware, madam, of your sister's distress, and its cause; I am aware, also, that I am honoured with a visit from two ladies of the highest consideration – Lady Bothwell and Lady Forester. If I could not distinguish them from the class of society which their present dress would indicate, there would be small possibility of my being able to gratify them by giving the information which they come to seek.'

'I can easily understand,' said Lady Bothwell . . .

'Pardon my boldness to interrupt you, milady,' cried the Italian; 'your ladyship was about to say that you could easily understand that I had got possession of your names by means of your domestic. But in thinking so, you do injustice to the fidelity of your servant, and, I may add, to the skill of one who is also not less your humble servant – Baptista Damiotti.'

'I have no intention to do either, sir,' said Lady Both-well, maintaining a tone of composure, though somewhat surprised, 'but the situation is something new to me. If you know who we are, you also know, sir, what brought us here.'

'Curiosity to know the fate of a Scottish gentleman of rank, now, or lately upon the Continent,' answered the seer; 'His name is Il Cavaliero Philippo Forester; a gentle-man who has the honour to be husband to this lady, and, with your ladyship's permission for using plain language, the misfortune not to value as it deserves that inestimable advantage.'

Lady Forester sighed deeply, and Lady Bothwell replied –

'Since you know our object without our telling it, the only question that remains is, whether you have the power to relieve my sister's anxiety?'

'I have, madam,' answered the Paduan scholar; 'but there is still a previous inquiry. Have you the courage to behold with your own eyes what the Cavaliero Philippo Forester is now doing? or will you take it on my report?"

'That question my sister must answer for herself,' said Lady Bothwell.

'With my own eyes will I endure to see whatever you have power to show me,' said Lady Forester, with the same determined spirit which had stimulated her since her resolution was taken upon this subject.

'There may be danger in it.'

'If gold can compensate the risk', said Lady Forester, taking out her purse.

'I do not such things for the purpose of gain,' answered the foreigner. 'I dare not turn my art to such a purpose. If I take the gold of the wealthy, it is but to bestow it on the poor; nor do I ever accept more than the sum I have already received from your servant. Put up your purse, madam; an adept needs not your gold.'

Lady Bothwell considering this rejection of her sister's offer as a mere trick of an empiric, to induce her to press a larger sum upon him, and willing that the scene should be commenced and ended, offered some gold in turn, observing that it was only to enlarge the sphere of his charity.

'Let Lady Bothwell enlarge the sphere of her own charity,' said the Paduan, 'not merely in giving of alms, in which I know she is not deficient, but in judging the character of others; and let her oblige Baptista Damiotti by believing him honest, till she shall discover him to be a knave. Do not be surprised, madam, if I speak in answer to your thoughts rather than your expressions, and tell me once more whether you have courage to look on what I am prepared to show?'

'I own, sir,' said Lady Bothwell, 'that your words strike me with some sense of fear; but whatever my sister desires to witness, I will not shrink from witnessing along with her.'

'Nay, the danger only consists in the risk of your resolution failing you. The sight can only last for the space of seven minutes; and should you interrupt the vision by speaking a single word, not only would the charm be broken, but some danger might result to the spectators. But if you can remain steadily silent for the seven minutes, your curiosity will be gratified without the slightest risk; and for this I will engage my honour."

Internally Lady Bothwell thought the security was but an indifferent one; but she suppressed the suspicion, as if she had believed that the adept, whose dark features wore a half-formed smile, could in reality read even her most secret reflections. A solemn pause then ensued, until Lady Forester gathered courage enough to reply to the physician, as he termed himself, that she would abide with firmness and silence the sight which he had promised to exhibit to them.

Upon this, he made them a low obeisance, and saying he went to matters to meet their wish, left the apartment. The two sisters, hand in hand, as if seeking by that close union to divert any danger which might threaten them, sat down on two seats in immediate contact with each other: Jemima seeking support in the manly and habitual courage of Lady Bothwell; and she, on the other hand, more agitated than she had expected, endeavouring to fortify herself by the desperate resolution which circumstances had forced her sister to assume. The one perhaps said to herself, that her sister never feared anything; and the other might reflect, that what so feeble a minded woman as Jemima did not fear, could not properly be a subject of apprehension to a person of firmness and resolution like herself.

In a few moments the thoughts of both were diverted from their own situation by a strain of music so singularly sweet and solemn, that, while it seemed calculated to avert or dispel any feeling unconnected with its harmony, increased, at the same time, the solemn excitation which the preceding interview was calculated to produce. The music was that of some instrument with which they were unacquainted; but circumstances afterwards led my ancestress to believe that it was that of the harmonica, which she heard at a much later period in life.

When these heaven-born sounds had ceased, a door opened in the upper end of the apartment, and they saw Damiotti, standing at the head of two or three steps, sign to them to advance. His dress was so different from that which he had worn a few minutes before, that they could hardly recognize him; and the deadly paleness of his countenance, and a certain stern rigidity of muscles, like that of one whose mind is made up to some strange and daring action, had totally changed the somewhat sarcastic expression with which he had previously regarded them both, and particularly Lady Bothwell. He was barefooted, excepting a species of sandals in the antique fashion; his legs were naked beneath the knees; above them he wore hose, and a doublet of dark crimson silk close to his body; and over that a flowing loose robe, something resembling a surplice, of snow-white linen; his throat and neck were uncovered, and his long, straight, black hair was carefully combed down at full length.

As the ladies approached at his bidding, he showed no gesture of that ceremonious courtesy of which he had been formerly lavish. On the contrary, he made the signal of advance with an air of command; and when, arm in arm, and with insecure steps, the sisters approached the spot where he stood, it was with a warning frown that he pressed his fingers to his lips, as if reiterating his condition of absolute silence, while, stalking before them, he led the way into the next apartment.

This was a large room, hung with black, as if for a funeral. At the upper end was a table, or rather a species of altar, covered with the same lugubrious colour, on which lay divers objects resembling the usual implements of sorcery. These objects were not indeed visible as they advanced into the apartment; for the light which displayed them, being only that of two expiring lamps, was extremely faint. The master – to use the Italian phrase for persons of this description – approached the upper end of the room with a genuflexion like that of a Catholic to the crucifix, and at the same time crossed himself. The ladies followed in silence, and arm in arm. Two or three low broad steps led to a platform in front of the altar, or what resembled such. Here the sage took his stand, and placed the ladies beside him, once more earnestly repeating by signs his injunctions of silence. The Italian then, extending his bare arm from under his linen vestment, pointed with his forefinger to five large flambeaux, or torches, placed on each side of the altar. They took fire successively at the approach of his hand, or rather of his finger, and spread a strong light through the room. By this the visitors could discern that, on the seeming altar, were disposed two naked swords laid crosswise; a large open book, which they conceived to be a copy of the Holy Scriptures, but in a language to them unknown; and beside this mysterious volume was placed a human skull. But what struck the sisters most was a very tall and broad mirror which occupied all the space behind the altar, and, illumined by the lighted torches, reflected the mysterious articles which were laid upon it.

The master then placed himself between the two ladies, and, pointing to the mirror, took each by the hand, but without speaking a syllable. They gazed intently on the polished and sable space to which he had directed their attention. Suddenly the surface assumed a new and singular appearance. It no longer simply reflected the objects before it, but, as if it had self-contained scenery of its own, objects began to appear within it, at first in a disorderly, indistinct, and miscellaneous manner, like form arranging itself out of chaos; at length, in distinct and defined shape and symmetry. It was thus that, after some shifting of light and darkness over the face of the wonderful glass, a long perspective of arches and columns began to arrange itself on its sides, and a vaulted roof on the upper part of it; till, after many oscillations, the whole vision gained a fixed and stationary appearance, representing the interior of a foreign church. The pillars were stately, and hung with scutcheons; the arches were lofty and magnificent; the floor was lettered with funeral inscriptions. But there were no separate shrines, no images, no display of chalice or crucifix on the altar. It was, therefore, a Protestant church upon the Continent. A clergyman, dressed in the Geneva gown and band, stood by the communion table, and with the Bible opened before him, and his clerk awaiting in the background, seemed prepared to perform some service of the church to which he belonged.

At length there entered the middle aisle of the building a numerous party, which appeared to be a bridal one, as a lady and gentleman walked first, hand in hand, followed by a large concourse of persons of both sexes, gaily, nay richly, attired. The bride, whose features they could distinctly see, seemed not more than sixteen years old, and extremely beautiful. The bridegroom, for some seconds, moved rather with his shoulder towards them, and his face averted; but his elegance of form and step struck the sisters at once with the same apprehension. As he turned his face suddenly, it was frightfully realized, and they saw, in the gay bridegroom before them, Sir Philip Forester. His wife uttered an imperfect exclamation, at the sound of which the whole scene stirred and seemed to separate.

'I could compare it to nothing,' said Lady Bothwell, while recounting the wonderful tale, 'but to the dispersion of the reflection offered by a deep and calm pool, when a stone is suddenly cast into it, and the shadows become dissipated and broken.' The master pressed both the ladies' hands severely, as if to remind them of their promise, and of the danger which they incurred. The exclamation died away on Lady Forester's tongue, without attaining perfect utterance, and the scene in the glass, after the fluctuation of a minute, again resumed to the eye its former appearance of a real scene, existing within the mirror, as if represented in a picture, save that the figures were movable instead of being stationary.

The representation of Sir Philip Forester, now distinctly visible in form and feature, was seen to lead on towards the clergyman that beautiful girl, who advanced at once with diffidence, and with a species of affectionate pride. In the meantime, and just as the clergyman had arranged the bridal company before him, and seemed about to commence the service, another group of persons, of whom two or three were officers, entered the church. They moved, at first, forward, as though they came to witness the bridal ceremony, but suddenly one of the officers, whose back was towards the spectators, detached himself from his companions, and rushed hastily towards the marriage party, when the whole of them turned towards him, as if attracted by some exclamation which had accompanied his advance. Suddenly the intruder drew his sword; the bridegroom unsheated his own, and made towards him; swords were also drawn by other individuals, both of the marriage party and of those who had last entered. They fell into a sort of confusion, the clergyman, and some elder and graver persons, labouring apparently to keep the peace, while the hotter spirits on both sides brandished their weapons. But now the period of brief space during which the soothsayer, as he pretended, was permitted to exhibit his art, was arrived. The fumes again mixed together, and dissolved gradually from observation; the vaults and columns of the church rolled asunder and disappeared; and the front of the mirror reflected nothing save the blazing torches, and the melancholy apparatus placed on the altar or table before it.

The doctor led the ladies, who greatly required his support, into the apartment from whence they came; where wine, essences, and other means of restoring suspended animation, had been provided during his absence. He motioned them to chairs, which they occupied in silence; Lady Forester, in particular, wringing her hands, and casting her eyes up to heaven, but without speaking a word, as if the spell had been still before her eyes.

'And what we have seen is even now acting?' said Lady Bothwell, collecting herself with difficulty.

'That,' answered Baptista Damiotti, 'I cannot justly, or with certainty, say. But it is either now acting, or has been acted, during a short space before this. It is the last remarkable transaction in which the Cavalier Forester has been engaged."

Lady Bothwell then expressed anxiety concerning her sister, whose altered countenance, and apparent unconsciousness of what passed around her, excited her apprehensions how it might be possible to convey her home.

'I have prepared for that,' answered the adept; 'I have directed the servant to bring your equipage as near to this place as the narrowness of the street will permit. Fear not for your sister; but give her, when you return home, this composing draught, and she will be better tomorrow morning. Few,' he added, in a melancholy tone, 'leave this house as well in health as they entered it. Such being the consequence of seeking knowledge by mysterious means. I leave you to judge the condition of those who have the power of gratifying such irregular curiosity. Farewell, and forget not the potion.'

'I will give her nothing that comes from you,' said Lady Bothwell; 'I have seen enough of your art already. Perhaps you would poison us both to conceal your own necromancy. But we are persons who want neither the means of making our wrongs known, nor the assistance of friends to right them.'

'You have had no wrongs from me, madam,' said the adept. 'You sought one who is little grateful for such honour. He seeks no one, and only gives responses to those who invite and call upon him. After all, you have but learned a little sooner the evil which you must still be doomed to endure. I hear your servant's step at the door, and will detain your ladyship and Lady Forester no longer. The next packet from the Continent will explain what you have already partly witnessed. Let it not, if I may advise, pass too suddenly into your sister's hands.'

So saying, he bid Lady Bothwell goodnight. She went, lighted by the adept, to the vestibule, where he hastily threw a black cloak over his singular dress, and opening the door entrusted his visitors to the care of the servant. It was with difficulty that Lady Bothwell sustained her sister to the carriage, though it was only twenty steps distant. When they arrived at home, Lady Forester required medical assistance. The physician of the family attended, and shook his head on feeling her pulse.

'Here has been,' he said, 'a violent and sudden shock on the nerves. I must know how it has happened.'

Lady Bothwell admitted they had visited the conjurer, and that Lady Forester had received some bad news respecting her husband, Sir Philip.

'That rascally quack would make my fortune were he to stay in Edinburgh,' said the graduate; 'This is the seventh nervous case I have heard of his making for me, and all by effect of terror.' He next examined the composing draught which Lady Bothwell had unconsciously brought in her hand, tasted it, and pronounced it very germane to the matter, and what would save an application to the apothecary. He then paused, and looking at Lady Bothwell very significantly, at length added, 'I suppose I must not ask your ladyship anything about this Italian warlock's proceedings?'

'Indeed, Doctor,' answered Lady Bothwell, 'I consider what passed as confidential, and though the man may be a rogue, yet, as we were fools enough to consult him, we should, I think, be honest to keep his counsel.'

'*May* be a knave – come,' said the doctor, 'I am glad to hear your ladyship allows such a possibility in anything that comes from Italy.'

'What comes from Italy may be as good as what comes from Hanover, Doctor. But you and I will remain good friends, and that it may be so, we will say nothing of Whig or Tory.'

'Not I,' said the doctor, receiving his fee and taking his hat; 'a Carolus serves my purpose as well as a Willielmus.

But I should like to know why old Lady Saint Ringan's, and all that set, go about wasting their decayed lungs in puffing this foreign fellow.'

'Aye – you had best set him down a Jesuit, as Scrub says.' On these terms they parted.

The poor patient – whose nerves, from an extraordinary state of tension, had at length become relaxed in as extraordinary a degree – continued to struggle with a sort of imbecility, the growth of superstitious terror, when the shocking tidings were brought from Holland, which fulfilled even her worst expectations.

They were sent by the celebrated Earl of Stair, and contained the melancholy event of a duel betwixt Sir Philip Forester and his wife's half-brother, Captain Falconer, of the Scotch-Dutch, as they were then called, in which the latter had been killed. The cause of quarrel rendered the incident still more shocking. It seemed that Sir Philip had left the army suddenly, in consequence of being unable to pay a very considerable sum which he had lost to another volunteer at play. He had changed his name, and taken up his residence at Rotterdam, where he had insinuated himself into the good graces of an ancient and rich burgomaster, and, by his handsome person and graceful manners, captivated the affections of his only child, a very young person, of great beauty, and the heiress of much wealth. Delighted with the specious attractions of his proposed son-in-law, the wealthy merchant – whose idea of the British character was too high to admit of his taking any precaution to acquire evidence of his condition and circumstances – gave his consent to the marriage. It was about to be celebrated in the principal church of the city, when it was interrupted by a singular occurrence.

Captain Falconer having been detached to Rotterdam to bring up a part of the brigade of Scottish auxiliaries who were in quarters there, a person of consideration in the

town, to whom he had been formerly known, proposed to
him for amusement to go to the high church, to see a
countryman of his own married to the daughter of a wealthy
burgomaster. Captain Falconer went accordingly, accompanied by his Dutch acquaintance with a party of his friends,
and two or three officers of the Scotch brigade. His
astonishment may be conceived when he saw his own
brother-in-law, a married man, on the point of leading to
the altar the innocent and beautiful creature, upon whom
he was about to practise a base and unmanly deceit. He pro-
claimed his villainy on the spot, and the marriage was interrupted of course. But against the opinion of more thinking
men, who considered Sir Philip Forester as having thrown
himself out of the rank of men of honour, Captain Falconer
admitted him to the privilege of such, accepted a challenge
from him, and in the rencounter received a mortal wound.
Such are the ways of heaven, mysterious in our eyes. Lady
Forester never recovered the shock of this dismal intelligence.

'And did this tragedy,' said I, 'take place exactly at the time
when the scene in the mirror was exhibited?'

'It is hard to be obliged to maim one's story,' answered
my aunt; 'but, to speak the truth, it happened some days
sooner than the apparition was exhibited.'

'And so there remained a possibility,' said I, 'that by
some secret and speedy communication the artist might
have received early intelligence of that incident.'

'The incredulous pretended so,' replied my aunt.

'What became of the adept?' demanded I.

'Why, a warrant came down shortly afterwards to arrest
him for high treason, as an agent of the Chevalier St.
George; and Lady Bothwell, recollecting the hints which
had escaped the doctor, an ardent friend of the Protestant
succession, did then call to remembrance, that this man was

chiefly *prôné* among the ancient matrons of her own political persuasion. It certainly seemed probable that intelligence from the Continent, which could easily have been transmitted by an active and powerful agent, might have enabled him to prepare such a scene of phantasmagoria as she herself witnessed. Yet there were so many difficulties in assigning a natural explanation that, to the day of her death, she remained in great doubt on the subject, and much disposed to cut the Gordian knot by admitting the existence of supernatural agency.'

'But, my dear aunt,' said I, 'what became of the man of skill?'

'Oh, he was too good a fortune-teller not to be able to foresee that his own destiny would be tragical if he waited the arrival of the man with the silver greyhound upon his sleeve. He made, as we say, a moonlight flitting, and was nowhere to be seen or heard of. Some noise there was about papers or letters found in the house, but it died away, and Doctor Baptista Damiotti was soon as little talked of as Galen or Hippocrates."

'And Sir Philip Forester,' said I, 'did he too vanish for ever from the public scene?'

'No,' replied my kind informer. 'He was heard of once more, and it was upon a remarkable occasion. It is said that we Scots, when there was such a nation in existence, have, among our full peck of virtues, one or two little barleycorns of vice. In particular, it is alleged that we rarely forgive, and never forget, any injuries received; that we used to make an idol of our resentment, as poor Lady Constance did of her grief; and are addicted, as Burns says, to 'nursing our wrath to keep it warm'. Lady Bothwell was not without feeling; and, I believe, nothing whatever, scarce the restoration of the Stuart line, could have happened so delicious to her feelings as an opportunity of being revenged on Sir Philip Forester, for the deep and double injury which had deprived her of a sister and of a brother. But nothing was heard or known till many a year had passed away.

At length – it was on a Fastern's E'en (Shrovetide) assembly, at which the whole fashion of Edinburgh attended, full and frequent, and when Lady Bothwell had a seat amongst the lady patronesses, that one of the attendants on the company whispered into her ear that a gentleman wished to speak with her in private.

'In private? and in an assembly-room? – he must be mad – Tell him to call upon me tomorrow morning.'

'I said so, my lady,' answered the man; 'but he desired me to give you this paper.'

She undid the billet, which was curiously folded and sealed. It only bore the words, *'On business of life and death,'* written in a hand which she had never seen before. Suddenly it occurred to her that it might concern the safety of some of her political friends; she therefore followed the messenger to a small apartment where the refreshments were prepared, and from which the general company was excluded. She found an old man, who, at her approach, rose up and bowed profoundly. His appearance indicated a broken constitution; and his dress, though sedulously rendered conforming to the etiquette of a ballroom, was worn and tarnished, and hung in folds about his emaciated person. Lady Bothwell was about to feel for her purse, expecting to get rid of the supplicant at the expense of a little money, but some fear of a mistake arrested her purpose. She therefore gave the man leisure to explain himself.

'I have the honour to speak with the Lady Bothwell?''

'I am Lady Bothwell: allow me to say that this is no time or place for long explanations. – What are your commands with me?'

'Your ladyship,' said the old man, 'had once a sister.'

'True; whom I loved as my own soul.'

'And a brother.'

'The bravest, the kindest, the most affectionate!' said Lady Bothwell.

'Both these beloved relatives you lost by the fault of an unfortunate man,' continued the stranger.

'By the crime of an unnatural, bloody-minded murderer,' said the lady.

'I am answered,' replied the old man, bowing, as if to withdraw.

'Stop, sir, I command you,' said Lady Bothwell. – 'Who are you that, at such a place and time, come to recall these horrible recollections? I insist upon knowing.'

'I am one who intends Lady Bothwell no injury; but, on the contrary, to offer her the means of doing a deed of Christian charity which the world would wonder at, and which heaven would reward; but I find her in no temper for such a sacrifice as I was prepared to ask.'

'Speak out, sir; what is your meaning?' said Lady Bothwell.

'The wretch that has wronged you so deeply,' rejoined the stranger, 'is now on his death-bed. His days have been days of misery, his nights have been sleepless hours of anguish – yet he cannot die without your forgiveness. His life has been an unremitting penance – yet he dares not part from his burden while your curses load his soul.'

'Tell him,' said Lady Bothwell sternly, 'to ask pardon of that Being whom he has so greatly offended; not of an erring mortal like myself. What could my forgiveness avail him?'

'Much,' answered the old man. 'It will be an earnest of that which he may then venture to ask from his Creator, lady, and from yours. Remember, Lady Bothwell, you too have a death-bed to look forward to; your soul may, all human souls must, feel the awe of facing the judgement-seat, with the wounds of an untented conscience, raw, and rankling – what thought would it be then that should whisper, "I have given no mercy, how then shall I ask it" '

'Man, whosoever thou mayest be,' replied Lady Bothwell, 'urge me not so cruelly. It would be but blasphemous hypocrisy to utter with my lips the words which every throb of my heart protests against. They would open the earth and give to light the wasted form of my sister – the bloody form of my murdered brother – forgive him? – Never, never!'

'Great God!' cried the old man, holding up his hands, 'is thus the worms which thou hast called out of dust obey the commands of their Maker? Farewell, proud and unforgiving woman. Exult that thou hast added to a death in want and pain the agonies of religious despair; but never again mock Heaven by petitioning for the pardon which thou hast refused to grant.'

He was turning from her.

'Stop,' she exclaimed; 'I will try; yes, I will try to pardon him.'

'Gracious lady,' said the old man, 'you will relieve the over-burdened soul, which dare not sever itself from its sinful companion of earth without being at peace with you. What do I know – your forgiveness may perhaps preserve for penitence the dregs of a wretched life.'

'Ha!' said the lady, as a sudden light broke on her, 'it is the villain himself.' And grasping Sir Philip Forester – for it was he, and no other – by the collar, she raised a cry of 'Murder, murder! Seize the murderer!'

At an exclamation so singular, in such a place, the company thronged into the apartment, but Sir Philip Forester was no longer there. He had forcibly extricated himself from Lady Bothwell's hold, and had run out of the apartment which opened on the landing-place of the stair. There seemed no escape in that direction, for there were several persons coming up the steps, and others descending. But the unfortunate man was desperate. He threw himself over the balustrade, and alighted safely in the lobby, through a leap of fifteen feet at least, then dashed into the street and was lost in darkness. Some of the Bothwell family made pursuit, and, had they come up with the fugitive, they might have perhaps slain him; for in those days men's blood ran warm in their veins. But the police did not interfere; the matter most criminal having happened long since, and in a foreign land. Indeed, it was always thought that this extraordinary scene originated in a hypocritical experiment, by which Sir Philip desired to ascertain whether he might return to his native country in safety from the resentment of a family which he had injured so deeply. As the result fell out so contrary to his wishes, he is believed to have returned to the Continent, and there died in exile.

So closed the tale of the MYSTERIOUS MIRROR.

from *The Keepsake* 1828.

WANDERING WILLIE'S TALE

WANDERING WILLIE'S TALE*

Y E maun have heard of Sir Robert Redgauntlet of that
Ilk, who lived in these parts before the dear years. The
country will lang mind him; and our fathers used to draw
breath thick if ever they heard him named. He was out wi'
the Hielandmen in Montrose's time; and again he was in the
hills wi' Glencairn in the saxteen hundred and fifty-twa;
and sae when King Charles the Second came in, wha was in
sic favour as the Laird of Redgauntlet? He was knighted at
Lonon court, wi' the King's ain sword; and being a redhot
prelatist, he came down here, rampauging like a lion, with
commissions of lieutenancy, and of lunacy for what I ken,
to put down a' the Whigs and Covenanters in the country.
Wild wark they made of it; for the Whigs were as dour as the
Cavaliers were fierce, and it was which should first tire the
other. Redgauntlet was aye for the stronghand; and his
name is kenn'd as wide in the country as Claverhouse's or
Tam Dalyell's. Glen, nor dargle, nor mountain, nor cave,
could hide the puir hill-folk when Redgauntlet was out
with bugle and bloodhound after them, as if they had been

*Glossary page 213

sae mony deer. And troth when they fand them, they didna mak muckle mair ceremony than a Hielandman wi' a roebuck – It was just, 'Will ye tak the test?' – if not, 'Make ready – present – fire!' – and there lay the recusant.

Far and wide was Sir Robert hated and feared. Men thought he had a direct compact with Satan – that he was proof against steel – and that bullets happed aff his buff-coat like hail-stanes from a hearth – that he had a mear that would turn a hare on the side of Carrifra-gawns – and muckle to the same purpose, of whilk mair anon. The best blessing they wared on him was, 'De'il scowp wi' Redgauntlet!' He wasna a bad master to his ain folk though, and was weel aneugh liked by his tenants; and as for the lackies and troopers that raid out wi' him to the persecutions, as the Whigs ca'ad these killing times, they wad hae drunken themsels blind to his health at ony time.

Now ye are to ken that my gudesire lived on Redgauntlet's grund – they ca' the place Primrose-Knowe. We had lived on the grund, and under the Redgauntlets, since the riding days, and lang before. It was a pleasant bit; and I think the air is callerer and fresher there than onywhere else in the country. It's a' deserted now; and I sat on the broken door-check three days since, and was glad I couldna see the plight the place was in; but that's a' wide o' the mark. There dwelt my gudesire, Steenie Steenson, a rambling, rattling chiel' he had been in his young days, and could play weel on the pipes; he was famous at "Hoopers and Girders" – a' Cumberland couldna touch him at "Jockie Lattin" – and he had the finest finger for the back-lill between Berwick and Carlisle. The like o' Steenie wasna the sort that they made Whigs o'. And so he became a Tory, as they ca' it, which we now ca' Jacobites, just out of a kind of needcessity, that he might belang to some side or other. He had nae ill-will to the Whig bodies, and likedna to see the blude rin, though, being obliged to follow Sir Robert in hunting and hosting, watching and warding, he saw muckle mischief, and maybe did some, that he couldna avoid.

Now Steenie was a kind of favourite with his master, and kenn'd a' the folks about the castle, and was often sent for to play the pipes when they were at their merriment. Auld Dougal MacCallum, the butler, that had followed Sir Robert through gude and ill, thick and thin, pool and stream, was specially fond of the pipes, and aye gae my gudesire his gude word wi' the Laird; for Dougal could turn his master round his finger.

Weel, round came the Revolution, and it had like to have broken the hearts baith of Dougal and his master. But the change was not a'thegether sae great as they feared, and other folk thought for. The Whigs made an unca crawing what they wad do with their auld enemies, and in special wi' Sir Robert Redgauntlet. But there were ower mony great folks dipped in the same doings, to make a spick and span new warld. So Parliament passed it a' ower easy; and Sir Robert, bating that he was held to hunting foxes instead of Covenanters, remained just the man he was. His revel was as loud, and his hall as weel lighted, as ever it had been, though maybe he lacked the fines of the non-conformists, that used to come to stock larder and cellar; for it is certain he began to be keener about the rents than his tenants used to find him before, and they behoved to be prompt to the rent-day, or else the Laird wasna pleased. And he was sic an awsome body, that naebody cared to anger him; for the oaths he swore, and the rage that he used to get into, and the looks that he put on, made men sometimes think him a deevil incarnate.

Weel, my gudesire was nae manager – no that he was a very great misguider – but he hadna the saving gift, and he got twa terms rent in arrear. He got the first brash at Whit-sunday put ower wi' fair words and piping; but when Martinmas came, there was a summons from the grund-officer to come wi' the rent on a day preceese, or else Steenie behoved to flitt. Sair wark he had to get the siller; but he was weel-freended, and at last he got the haill scraped thegether – a thousand merks – the maist of it was from a neighbour they ca'd Laurie Lapraik – a sly tod. Laurie had walth o' gear – could hunt wi' the hound and rin wi' the hare – and be Whig or Tory, saunt or sinner, as the wind stood. He was a professor in this Revolution warld, but he liked an orra sound and a tune on the pipes weel aneugh at a bye-time; and abune a', he thought he had gude security for the siller he lent my gudesire over the stocking at Primrose-Knowe.

Away trots my gudesire to Redgauntlet Castle wi' a heavy purse and a light heart, glad to be out of the Laird's danger. Weel, the first thing he learned at the Castle was, that Sir Robert had fretted himsell into a fit of the gout, because he did not appear before twelve o'clock. It wasna a'thegether for sake of the money, Dougal thought; but because he didna like to part wi' my gudesire aff the grund. Dougal was glad to see Steenie, and brought him into the great oak parlour, and there sat the Laird his leesome lane, excepting that he had beside him a great, ill-favoured jackanape, that was a special pet of his; a cankered beast it was, and mony an ill-natured trick it played – ill to please it was, and easily angered – ran about the haill castle, chattering and yowling, and pinching, and biting folk, specially before ill-weather, or disturbances in the state. Sir Robert ca'ed it Major Weir, after the warlock that was burned; and few folk liked either the name or the conditions of the creature – they thought there was something in it by ordinar – and my gudesire was not just easy in mind when the door shut on him, and he saw himself in the room wi' naebody but the Laird, Dougal MacAllum, and the Major, a thing that hadna chanced to him before.

Sir Robert sat, or, I should say, lay, in a great armed

chair, wi' his grand velvet gown, and his feet on a cradle; for he had baith gout and gravel, and his face looked as gash and ghastly as Satan's. Major Weir sat opposite to him, in a red-laced coat, and the Laird's wig on his head; and aye as Sir Robert girned wi' pain, the jackanape girned too, like a sheep's-head between a pair of tangs – an ill-faur'd, fearsome couple they were. The Laird's buff-coat was hung on a pin behind him, and his broadsword and his pistols within reach; for he keepit up the auld fashion of having the weapons ready, and a horse saddled day and night, just as he used to do when he was able to loup on horseback, and away after ony of the hill-folk he could get speerings of. Some said it was for fear of the Whigs taking vengeance, but I judge it was just his auld custom – he wasna gien to fear onything. The rental-book, wi' its black cover and brass clasps, was lying beside him; and a book of sculduddry sangs was put betwixt the leaves, to keep it open at the place where it bore evidence against the Goodman of Primrose-Knowe, as behind the hand with his mails and duties. Sir Robert gave my gudesire a look, as if he would have withered his heart in his bosom. Ye maun ken he had a way of bending his brows, that men saw the visible mark of a horse-shoe in his forehead, deep-dinted, as if it had been stamped there.

'Are ye come light-handed, ye son of a toom whistle?' said Sir Robert. 'Zounds! if you are. . . .'

My gudesire, with as gude a countenance as he could put on, made a leg, and placed the bag of money on the table wi' a dash, like a man that does something clever. The Laird drew it to him hastily – 'Is it all here, Steenie, man?'

'Your honour will find it right,' said my gudesire.

'Here, Dougal,' said the Laird, 'gie Steenie a tass of brandy down stairs, till I count the siller and write the receipt.'

But they werena weel out of the room, when Sir Robert

gied a yelloch that garr'd the castle rock. Back ran Dougal – in flew the livery-men – yell on yell gied the Laird, ilk ane mair awfu' than the ither. My gudesire knew not whether to stand or flee, but he ventured back into the parlour, where a' was gaun hirdy-girdie – naebody to say 'come in' or 'gae out'. Terribly the Laird roared for cauld water to his feet, and wine to cool his throat; and, Hell, hell, hell, and its flames, was aye the word in his mouth. They brought him water, and when they plunged his swoln feet into the tub, he cried out it was burning; and folk say that it *did* bubble and sparkle like a seething cauldron. He flung the cup at Dougal's head, and said he had given him blood instead of burgundy; and, sure aneugh, the lass washed clottered blood aff the carpet the neist day. The jackanape they ca'd Major Weir, it jibbered and cried as if it was mocking its master; my gudesire's head was like to turn – he forgot baith siller and receipt, and down stairs he banged; but as he ran, the shrieks came faint and fainter; there was a deep-drawn shivering groan, and word gaed through the Castle, that the Laird was dead.

Weel, away came my gudesire, wi' his finger in his mouth, and his best hope was, that Dougal had seen the money-bag, and heard the Laird speak of writing the receipt. The young Laird, now Sir John, came from Edinburgh, to see things put to rights. Sir John and his father never gree'd weel – he had been bred an advocate, and afterwards sat in the last Scots Parliament and voted for the Union, having gotten, it was thought, a rug of the compensations – if his father could have come out of his grave, he would have brained him for it on his awn hearthstane. Some thought it was easier counting with the auld rough Knight than the fair-spoken young ane – but mair of that anon.

Dougal MacCallum, poor body, neither grat nor graned, but gaed about the house looking like a corpse, but directing, as was his duty, a' the order of the grand funeral.

Now, Dougal looked aye waur and waur when night was coming, and was aye the last to gang to his bed, whilk was in a little round just opposite the chamber of dais, whilk his master occupied while he was living, and where he now lay in as they ca-ad it, well-a-day! The night before the funeral, Dougal could keep his awn counsel nae langer; he came doun with his proud spirit, and fairly asked auld Hutcheon to sit in his room with him for an hour. When they were in the round, Dougal took ae tass of brandy to himsel, and gave another to Hutcheon, and wished him all health and lang life, and said that, for himsel, he wasna lang for this world; for that, every night since Sir Robert's death, his silver call had sounded from the state chamber, just as it used to do at nights in his lifetime, to call Dougal to help to turn him in his bed. Dougal said, that being alone with the dead on that floor of the tower, (for naebody cared to wake Sir Robert Redgauntlet like another corpse,) he had never daured to answer the call, but that now his conscience checked him for neglecting his duty; for, "though death breaks service," said MacCallum, 'it shall never break my service to Sir Robert; and I will answer his next whistle, so be you will stand by me, Hutcheon.'

Hutcheon had nae will to the wark, but he had stood by Dougal in battle and broil, and he wad not fail him at this pinch; so down the carles sat over a stoup of brandy, and Hutcheon, who was something of a clerk, would have read a chapter of the Bible; but Dougal would hear naething but a blaud of Davie Lindsay, whilk was the waur preparation.

When midnight came, and the house was quiet as the grave, sure aneugh the silver whistle sounded as sharp and shrill as if Sir Robert was blowing it, and up got the twa auld serving-men, and tottered into the room where the dead man lay. Hutcheon saw aneugh at the first glance; for there were torches in the room, which shewed him the foul fiend, in his ain shape, sitting on the Laird's coffin! Over he cowped as if he had been dead. He could not tell how lang he lay in a trance at the door, but when he gathered himself, he cried on his neighbour, and getting no answer, raised the house, when Dougal was found lying dead within twa steps of the bed where his master's coffin was placed. As for the whistle, it was gaen anes and aye; but mony a time was it heard on the top of the house in the bartizan, and amang the auld chimnies and turrets, where the howlets have their nests. Sir John hushed the matter up, and the funeral passed over without mair bogle-wark.

But when a' was over, and the Laird was beginning to settle his affairs, every tenant was called up for his arrears, and my gudesire for the full sum that stood against him in the rental-book. Weel, away he trots to the Castle, to tell his story, and there he is introduced to Sir John, sitting in his father's chair, in deep mourning, with weepers and hanging cravat, and a small walking rapier by his side, instead of the auld broad-sword that had a hundred-weight of steel about it, what with blade, chape, and basket-hilt. I have heard their communing so often tauld ower, that I almost think I was there mysell, though I couldna be born at the time. (In fact, Alan, my companion mimicked, with a good deal of humour, the flattering, conciliating tone of the tenant's address, and the hypocritical melancholy of the Laird's reply. His grandfather, he said, had, while he spoke, his eye fixed on the rental-book, as if it were a mastiff-dog that he was afraid would spring up and bite him.)

'I wuss ye joy, sir, of the head-seat, and the white loaf, and the braid lairdship. Your father was a kind man to friends and followers; muckle grace to you, Sir John, to fill his shoon – his boots, I suld say, for he seldom wore shoon, unless it were muils when he had the gout.'

'Ay, Steenie,' quoth the Laird, sighing deeply, and putting his napkin to his een, 'his was a sudden call, and he will be missed in the country; no time to set his house in order – weel prepared God-ward, no doubt, which is the root of the matter – but left us behind a tangled hesp to wind, Steenie. – Hem! hem! We maun go to business, Steenie; much to do, and little time to do it in.'

Here he opened the fatal volume; I have heard of a thing they call Doomsday-book – I am clear it has been a rental of back-ganging tenants.

'Stephen,' said Sir John, still in the same soft, sleekit tone of voice – 'Stephen Stevenson, or Steenson, ye are down here for a year's rent behind the hand – due at last term.'

Stephen. 'Please your honour, Sir John, I paid it to your father.'

Sir John. 'Ye took a receipt then, doubtless, Stephen; and can produce it?'

Stephen. 'Indeed I hadna time, an it like your honour; for nae sooner had I set doun the siller, and just as his honour, Sir Robert, that's gaen, drew it till him to count it, and write out the receipt, he was ta'en wi' the pains that removed him.'

'That was unlucky,' said Sir John, after a pause. 'But ye maybe paid it in the presence of somebody. I wan but a *talis qualis* evidence, Stephen. I would go ower strictly to work with no poor man.'

Stephen. 'Troth, Sir John, there was naebody in the room but Dougal MacCallum the butler. But, as your honour kens, he has e'en followed his auld master.'

'Very unlucky again, Stephen,' said Sir John, without altering his voice a single note. 'The man to whom ye paid the money is dead – and the man who witnessed the payment is dead too – and the siller, which should have been to the fore, is neither seen nor heard tell of in the repositories. How am I to believe a' this?'

Stephen. 'I dinna ken, your honour; but there is a bit

memorandum note of the very coins; for, God help me! I had to borrow out of twenty purses; and I am sure that ilk man there set down will take his grit oath for what purpose I borrowed the money.'

Sir John. 'I have little doubt ye *borrowed* the money, Steenie. It is the *payment* that I want to have some proof of.'

Stephen. 'The siller maun be about the house, Sir John. And since your honour never got it, and his honour that was canna have taen it wi' him, maybe some of the family may have seen it.'

Sir John. 'We will examine the servants, Stephen; that is but reasonable.'

But lackey and lass, and page and groom, all denied stoutly that they had ever seen such a bag of money as my gudesire described. What was waur, he had unluckily not mentioned to any living soul of them his purpose of paying his rent. Ae quean had noticed something under his arm, but she took it for the pipes.

Sir John Redgauntlet ordered the servants out of the room, and then said to my gudesire, 'Now, Steenie, ye see you have fair play; and, as I have little doubt ye ken better where to find the siller than ony other body, I beg, in fair terms, and for your own sake, that you will end this fasherie; for, Stephen, ye maun pay or flitt.'

'The Lord forgie your opinion,' said Stephen, driven almost to his wits' end – 'I am an honest man.'

'So am I, Stephen,' said his honour; 'and so are all the folks in the house, I hope. But if there be a knave amongst us, it must be he that tells the story he cannot prove.' He paused, and then added, mair sternly, 'If I understand your trick, sir, you want to take advantage of some malicious reports concerning things in this family, and particularly respecting my father's sudden death, thereby to cheat me out of the money, and perhaps take away my character, by insinuating that I have received the rent I am demanding. –

Where do you suppose this money to be? – I insist upon knowing.'

My gudesire saw everything look so muckle against him, that he grew nearly desperate – however, he shifted from one foot to another, looked to every corner of the room, and made no answer.

'Speak out, sirrah,' said the Laird, assuming a look of his father's, a very particular ane, which he had when he was angry – it seemed as if the wrinkles of his frown made that self-same fearful shape of a horse's shoe in the middle of his brow; – 'Speak out, sir! I *will* know your thoughts; do you suppose that I have this money?'

'Far be it frae me to say so,' said Stephen.

'Do you charge any of my people with having taken it?'

'I wad be laith to charge them that may be innocent,' said my gudesire; 'and if there by any one that is guilty, I have nae proof.'

'Somewhere the money must be, if there is a word of truth in your story,' said Sir John; 'I ask where you think it is – and demand a correct answer?'

'In hell, if you will have my thoughts of it,' said my gudesire, driven to extremity, – 'in hell! with your father and his silver whistle.'

Down the stairs he ran, (for the parlour was nae place for him after such a word) and he heard the Laird swearing blood and wounds behind him, as fast as ever did Sir Robert. and roaring for the baillie and the baron-officer.

Away rode my gudesire to his chief creditor, (him they ca'd Laurie Lapraik,) to try if he could make onything out of him; but when he tauld his story, he got but the warst word in his wame – thief, beggar, and dyvour, were the safest terms; and to the boot of these hard terms, Laurie brought up the auld story of his dipping his hand in the blood of God's saints, just as if a tenant could have helped riding with the Laird, and that a laird like Sir Robert Redgauntlet. My gudesire was, by this time, far beyond the bounds of patience, and, while he and Laurie were at de'il speed the liars, he was wanchancie aneugh to abuse his doctrine was weel as the man, and said things that gar'd folks flesh grew that heard them; – he wasna just himsell, and he had lived wi' a wild set in his day.

At last they parted, and my gudesire was to ride hame through the wood of Pitmarkie, that is a' fou of black firs, as they say. – I ken the wood, but the firs may be black or white for what I can tell. – At the entry of the wood there is a wild common, and on the edge of the common, a little lonely change-house, that was keepit then by an ostler-wife, they suld hae ca'd her Tibbie Faw, and there puir Steenie cried for a mutchkin of brandy, for he had had no refreshment the hail day. Tibbie was earnest wi him to take a bite of meat, but he couldna think o't, nor would he take his foot out of the stirrup, and took off the brandy wholely at twa draughts, and named a toast at each: – the first was, the memory of Sir Robert Redgauntlet, and might he never lie quiet in his grave till he had righted his poor bond-tenant; and the second was, a health to Man's Enemy, if he would but get him back the pock of siller, or tell him what came o't, for he saw the hail world was like to regard him as a thief and a cheat, and he took that waur than even the ruin of his house and hauld.

On he rode, little caring where. It was a dark night turned, and the trees made it yet darker, and he let the beast take its ain road through the wood; when, all of a sudden, from tired and wearied that it was before, the nag began to spring, and flee, and stend, that my gudesire could hardly keep the saddle—Upon the whilk, a horseman, suddenly riding up beside him, said, 'That's a mettle beast of yours, freend; will you sell him?'—So saying, he touched the horse's neck with his riding-wand, and it fell into its auld heigh-ho of a stumbling trot; 'But his spunk's soon out of him, I think,' continued the stranger, 'and that is like mony a man's courage, that thinks he wad do great things till he come to the proof.'

My gudesire scarce listened to this, but spurred his horse, with 'Gude e'en to you, freend.'

But it's like the stranger was ane that does na lightly yield his point; for, ride as Steenie liked, he was aye beside him at the self-same pace. At last my gudesire, Steenie Steenson, grew half angry; and, to say the truth, half feared.

'What is that ye want with me, freend?' he said. 'If ye be a robber, I have nae money; if ye be a leal man, wanting company, I have nae heart to mirth or speaking; and if ye want to ken the road, I scarce ken it mysell.'

'If you will tell me your grief,' said the stranger, 'I am one that, though I have been sair miscaad in the world, am the only hand for helping my friends.'

So my gudesire, to ease his ain heart, mair than from any hope of help, told him the story from beginning to end.

'It's a hard pinch,' said the stranger; 'but I think I can help you.'

'If you could lend the money, sir, and take a lang day—I ken nae other help on earth,' said my gudesire.

'But there may be some under the earth,' said the stranger. 'Come, I'll be frank wi' you; I could lend you the money on bond, but you would maybe scruple my terms. Now, I can tell you, that your auld Laird is disturbed in his grave by your curses, and the wailing of your family, and—if ye daur venture to go to see him, he will give you the receipt.'

My gudesire's hair stood on end at this proposal, but he thought his companion might be some humoursome chield that was trying to frighten him, and might end with lending him the money. Besides, he was bauld wi' brandy, and desperate wi' distress; and he said, he had courage to go to the gate of hell, and a step farther, for that receipt.—The stranger laughed.

Weel, they rode on through the thickest of the wood, when, all of a sudden, the horse stopped at the door of a great house; and, but that he knew the place was ten miles off, my father would have thought he was at Redgauntlet Castle. They rode into the outer-yard, through the muckle faulding yetts, and aneath the auld portcullis; and the whole front of the house was lighted, and there were pipes and fiddles, and as much dancing and deray within as used to be in Sir Robert's house at Pace and Yule, and such high seasons. They lap off, and my gudesire, as seemed to him, fastened his horse to the very ring he had tied him to that morning, when he gaed to wait on the young Sir John.

'God!' said my father, 'if Sir Robert's death be but a dream!'

He knocked at the ha' door, just as he wont, and his auld acquaintance, Dougal MacCallum, just after his wont, too,—came to open the door, and said, 'Piper Steenie, are ye there, lad? Sir Robert has been crying for you.'

My gudesire was like a man in a dream – he looked for the stranger, but he was gaen for the time. At last, he just tried to say, 'Ha! Dougal Driveower, are ye living? I thought ye had been dead.'

'Never fash yoursell wi' me,' said Dougal, 'but look to yoursell; and see ye tak naething frae onybody here, neither meat, drink, or siller, except just the receipt that is your ain.'

So saying, he led the way out through halls and trances that were weel kenn'd to my gudesire, and into the auld oak parlour; and there was as much singing of profane sangs, and birling of red wine, and speaking blasphemy and sculduddry, as had ever been in Redgauntlet Castle when it was at the blythest.

But, Lord take us in keeping! what a set of ghastly revellers they were that sat round that table!—My gudesire kenn'd mony that had long before gane to their place. There was the fierce Middleton, and the dissolute Rothes, and the crafty Lauderdale; and Dalyell, with his bald head and a beard to his girdle; and Earlshall, with Cameron's blude on his hand; and wild Bonshaw, that tied blessed Mr. Cargill's limbs till the blude sprung; and Dumbarton Douglas, the twice-turned traitor baith to country and king. There was the Bluidy Advocate MacKenyie, who, for his wordly wit and wisdom, had been to the rest as a god. And there was Claverhouse, as beautiful as when he lived, with his long, dark, curled locks, streaming down to his laced buff-coat, and his left hand always on his right spule-blade, to hide the wound that the silver bullet had made. He sat apart from them all, and looked at them with a melancholy, haughty countenance; while the rest hallooed, and sung, and laughed, that the room rang. But their smiles were fearfully contorted from time to time; and their laughter passed into such wild sounds, as made my gudesire's very nails grow blue, and chilled the marrow in his banes.

They that waited at the table were just the wicked serving-men and troopers, that had done their work and wicked bidding on earth. There was the Lang Lad of the Nether-town, that helped to take Argyle; and the Bishop's summoner, that they called the De'il's Rattle-bag; and the wicked guardsmen, in their laced coats; and the savage Highland Amorites, that shed blood like water; and many a proud serving-man, haughty of heart and bloody of hand, cringing to the rich, and making them wickeder than they would be; grinding the poor to powder, when the rich had broken them to fragments. And mony, mony mair were coming and ganging, a' as busy in their vocation as if they had been alive.

Sir Robert Redgauntlet, in the midst of a' this fearful riot, cried, wi' a voice like thunder, on Steenie Piper, to come to the board-head where he was sitting; his legs stretched out before him, and swathed up with flannel, with his holster pistols aside him, and the great broad-sword rested against his chair, just as my gudesire had seen him the last time upon earth—the very cushion for the jackanape was close to him, but the creature itsell was not there—it wasna its hour, it's likely; for he heard them say as he came forward, 'Is not the Major come yet?' And another answered, 'The jackanape will be here betimes the morn.' And when my gudesire came forward, Sir Robert, or his ghaist, or the deevil in his likeness, said, 'Weel, piper, hae ye settled wi' my son for the year's rent?'

With much ado my father gat breath to say, that Sir John would not settle without his honour's receipt.

'Ye shall hae that for a tune of the pipes, Steenie,' said the appearance of Sir Robert – 'Play us up "Weel hoddled, Luckie."'

Now this was a tune my gudesire learned frae a warlock, that heard it when they were worshipping Satan at their meetings; and my gudesire had sometimes played it at the ranting suppers in Redgauntlet Castle, but never very willingly; and now he grew cauld at the very name of it, and said, for excuse, he hadna his pipes wi' him.

'MacCallum, ye limb of Beelzebub,' said the fearfu' Sir Robert, 'bring Steenie the pipes that I am keeping for him!'

MacCallum brought a pair of pipes might have served the piper of Donald of the Isles. But he gave my gudesire a nudge as he offered them; and looking secretly and closely, Steenie saw that the chanter was of steel, and heated to a white heat; so he had fair warning not to trust his fingers with it. So he excused himself again, and said, he was faint and frightened, and had not wind aneugh to fill the bag.

'Then ye maun eat and drink, Steenie,' said the figure; 'for we do little else here; and it's ill speaking between a fou man and a fasting.'

Now these were the very words that the bloody Earl of Douglas said to keep the King's messenger in hand, while he cut the head off MacLellan of Bombie, at the Threave

Castle; and that put Steenie mair and mair on his guard. So he spoke up like a man, and said he came neither to eat, or drink, or make minstrelsy; but simply for his ain – to ken what was come o' the money he had paid, and to get a discharge for it; and he was so stout-hearted by this time, that he charged Sir Robert for conscience-sake—(he had no power to say the holy name)—and as he hoped for peace and rest, to spread no snares for him, but just to give him his ain.

The appearance gnashed its teeth and laughed, but it took from a large pocket-book the receipt, and handed it to Steenie. 'Here is your receipt, ye pitiful cur; and for the money, my dog-whelp of a son may go look for it in the Cat's Cradle.'

My gudesire uttered mony thanks, and was about to retire, when Sir Robert roared aloud, 'Stop though, thou sack-doudling son of a whore! I am not done with thee. HERE we do nothing for nothing; and you must return on this very day twelvemonth, to pay your master the homage that you owe me for my protection.'

My father's tongue was loosed of a suddenty, and he said aloud, 'I refer mysell to God's pleasure, and not to yours.'

He had no sooner uttered the word than all was dark around him; and he sunk on the earth with such a sudden shock, that he lost both breath and sense.

How lang Steenie lay there, he could not tell; but when he came to himsell, he was lying in the auld kirkyard of Redgauntlet parishine, just at the door of the family aisle, and the scutcheon of the auld knight, Sir Robert, hanging over his head. There was a deep morning fog on grass and gravestone around him, and his horse was feeding quietly beside the minister's twa cows. Steenie would have thought the whole was a dream, but he had the receipt in his hand, fairly written and signed by the auld Laird; only the last letters of his name were a little disorderly, written like one seized with sudden pain.

Sorely troubled in his mind, he left that dreary place, rode through the mist to Redgauntlet Castle, and with much ado he got speech of the Laird. 'Well, you dyvour bankrupt,' was the first word, 'have you brought me my rent?'

'No,' answered my gudesire, 'I have not; but I have brought your honour Sir Robert's receipt for it.'

'How, sirrah?—Sir Robert's receipt!—You told me he had not given you one.'

'Will your honour please to see if that bit line is right?'

Sir John looked at every line, and at every letter, with much attention; and at last, at the date, which my gudesire had not observed,—'*From my appointed place,*' he read, '*this twenty-fifth of November.*'—'What!—That is yesterday! Villain, thou must have gone to hell for this!'

'I got it from your honour's father—whether he be in heaven or hell, I know not,' said Steenie.

'I will delate you for a warlock to the Privy Council!' said Sir John. 'I will send you to your master, the devil, with the help of a tar-barrel and a torch!'

'I intend to delate mysell to the Presbytery,' said Steenie, 'and tell them all I have seen last night, whilk are things fitter for them to judge of than a borrel man like me.'

Sir John paused, composed himself, and desired to hear the full history; and my gudesire told it him from point to point, as I have told it you—word for word, neither more nor less.

Sir John was silent again for a long time, and at last he said, very composedly, 'Steenie, this story of yours concerns the honour of many a noble family besides mine; and if it be a leasing-making, to keep yourself out of my danger, the least you can expect is to have a red-hot iron driven through your tongue, and that will be as bad as scauding your fingers wi' a red-hot chanter. But yet it may be true, Steenie; and if the money cast up, I will not know what to think of it.—But where shall we find the Cat's Cradle? There are cats enough about the old house, but I think they kitten without the ceremony of bed or cradle.'

'We were best ask Hutcheon,' said my gudesire; 'he kens a' the odd corners about as weel as—another serving-man that is now gane, and that I wad not like to name.'

Aweel, Hutcheon, when he was asked, told them, that a ruinous turret, lang disused, next to the clock-house, only accessible by a ladder, for the opening was on the outside, and far above the battlements, was called of old the Cat's Cradle.

'There will I go immediately,' said Sir John; and he took (with what purpose, Heaven kens,) one of his father's pistols from the hall-table, where they had lain since the night he died, and hastened to the battlements.

It was a dangerous place to climb, for the ladder was auld and frail, and wanted ane or twa rounds. However, up got Sir John, and entered at the turret door, where his body stopped the only little light that was in the bit turret. Something flees at him wi' a vengeance, maist dang him back ower—bang gaed the knight's pistol, and Hutcheon, that held the ladder, and my gudesire that stood beside him, hears a loud skelloch. A minute after, Sir John flings the body of the jackanape down to them, and cries that the siller is fund, and that they should come up and help him. And there was the bag of siller sure aneugh, and mony orra things besides, that had been missing for mony a day. And Sir John, when he had riped the turret weel, led my gudesire into the dining-parlour, and took him by the hand, and spoke kindly to him, and said he was sorry he should have doubted his word, and that he would hereafter be a good master to him, to make amends.

'And now, Steenie,' said Sir John, 'although this vision of yours tends, on the whole, to my father's credit, as an honest man, that he should, even after his death, desire to see justice done to a poor man like you, yet you are sensible that ill-dispositioned men might make bad constructions upon it, concerning his soul's health. So, I think, we had better lay the hail dirdum on that ill-deedie creature, Major Weir, and say naething about your dream in the wood of Pitmurkie. You had taken ower mickle brandy to be very certain about onything; and, Steenie, this receipt, (his hand shook while he held it out)—it's but a queer kind of document, and we will do best, I think, to put it quietly in the fire.'

'Od, but for as queer as it is, it's a' the voucher I have for my rent,' said my gudesire, who was afraid, it may be, of losing the benefit of Sir Robert's discharge.

'I will bear the contents to your credit in the rental-book, and give you a discharge under my own hand,' said Sir John, 'and that on the spot. And, Steenie, if you can hold your tongue about this matter, you shall sit, from this term downward, at an easier rent.'

'Mony thanks to your honour,' said Steenie, who saw easily in what corner the wind sat; 'doubtless I will be conformable to all your honour's commands; only I would willingly speak wi' some powerful minister on the subject, for I do not like the sort of soumons of appointment whilk you honour's father——'

'Do not call the phantom my father!' said Sir John, interrupting him.

'Weel, then, the thing that was so like him,'—said my gudesire; 'he spoke of my coming back to him this time twelvemonth, and it's a weight on my conscience.'

'Aweel, then,' said Sir John, 'if you be so much distressed in mind, you may speak to our minister of the parish; he is a douce man, regards the honour of our family, and the mair that he may look for some patronage from me.'

Wi' that, my father readily agreed that the receipt should be burnt, and the Laird threw it into the chimney with his ain hand. Burn it would not for them, though; but away it flew up the lumm, wi'a lang train of sparks at its tail, and a hissing noise like a squib.

My gudesire gaed down to the Manse, and the minister, when he had heard the story, said, it was his real opinion, that though my gudesire had gaen very far in tampering with dangerous matters, yet, as he had refused the devil's arles, (for such was the offer of meat and drink), and had refused to do homage by piping at his bidding, he hoped, that if he held a circumspect walk hereafter, Satan could take little advantage by what was come and gane. And, indeed, my gudesire, of his ain accord, lang forswore baith the pipes and brandy—it was not even till the year was out, and the fatal day passed, that he would so much as take the fiddle, or drink usquebaugh or tippenny.

Sir John made up his story about the jackanape as he liked himself; and some believe till this day there was no more in the matter than the filching nature of the brute. Indeed ye'll no hinder some to threap, that it was nane o' the Auld Enemy that Dougal and my gudesire saw in the Laird's room, but only that wanchancy creature, the Major, capering on the coffin; and that, as to the blawing on the Laird's whistle that was heard after he was dead, the filthy brute could do that as weel as the Laird himsell, if no better. But Heaven kens the truth, whilk first came out by the minister's wife, after Sir John and her ain gudeman were baith in the moulds. And then my gudesire, wha was failed in his limbs, but not in his judgement or memory—at least nothing to speak of—was obliged to tell the real narrative to his friends, for the credit of his gude name. He might else have been charged for a warlock.'

from *Redgauntlet* 1824

THE TWO DROVERS

THE TWO DROVERS

1

IT was the day after Doune Fair when my story commences. It had been a brisk market, several dealers had attended from the northern and midland counties in England, and English money had flown so merrily about as to gladden the hearts of the Highland farmers. Many large droves were about to set off for England, under the protection of their owners, or of the topsmen whom they employed in the tedious, laborious, and responsible office of driving the cattle for many hundred miles, from the market where they had been purchased, to the fields or farm-yards where they were to be fattened for the shambles.

The Highlanders, in particular, are masters of this difficult trade of driving, which seems to suit them as well as the trade of war. It affords exercise for all their habits of patient endurance and active exertion. They are required to know perfectly the drove roads, which lie over the wildest tracts of the country, and to avoid as much as possible the highways, which distress the feet of the bullocks, and the turnpikes, which annoy the spirit of the drover; whereas, on the broad green or grey track, which leads across the path-less moor, the herd not only move at ease and without taxation, but, if they mind their business, may pick up a mouthful of food by the way. At night, the drivers usually sleep along with their cattle, let the weather be what it will, and many of these hardy men do not once rest under a roof during a journey on foot from Lochaber to Lincolnshire. They are paid very highly, for the trust reposed is of the last importance, as it depends on their prudence, vigilance, and honesty, whether the cattle reach the final market in good order, and afford a profit to the grazier. But as they maintain themselves at their own expense, they are especially economical in that particular. At the period we speak of, a Highland drover was victualled for his long and toilsome journey with a few handfuls of oatmeal, and two or three onions, renewed from time to time, and a ram's horn filled with whisky, which he used regularly, but sparingly, every night and morning. His dirk, or *skene-dhu* (black-knife), so worn as to be concealed beneath the arm, or by the folds of the plaid, was his only weapon, excepting the cudgel with which he directed the movement of the cattle. A highlander was never so happy as on these occasions. There was a variety in the whole journey, which exercised the Celt's natural curiosity and love of motion; there were the constant change of place and scene, the petty adventures incidental to the traffic, and the intercourse with the various farmers, graziers, and traders, intermingled with occasional merry-makings, not the less acceptable to Donald that they were void of expense—and there was the consciousness of superior skill for the Highlander, a child amongst flocks, is a prince amongst herds, and his natural habits induce him to disdain the shepherd's slothful life, so that he feels himself nowhere more at home than when following a gallant drove of his country cattle in the character of their guardian.

Of the number who left Doune in the morning, and with the purpose we described, not a *Glunamie* of them all cocked his bonnet more briskly, or gartered his tartan hose under knee over a pair of more promising spiogs(legs) than did Robin Oig M'Combich, called familiarly Robin Oig, that is, Young, or the Lesser, Robin. Though small of stature as the epithet Oig implies, and not very strongly limbed, he was as light and alert as one of the deer of his mountains. He had an elasticity of step which, in the course of a long march, made many a stout fellow envy him; and the manner in which he busked his plaid and adjusted his bonnet, argued a consciousness that so smart a John Highlandman as himself would not pass unnoticed among the Lowland lasses. The ruddy cheek, red lips, and white teeth, set off a countenance which had gained by exposure to the weather a healthful and hardy rather than a rugged hue. If Robin Oig did not laugh, or even smile frequently, as indeed is not the practice among his countrymen, his bright eyes usually gleamed from under his bonnet with an expression of cheerfulness ready to be turned into mirth.

The departure of Robin Oig was an incident in the little town, in and near which he had many friends, male and female. He was a topping person in his way, transacted considerable business on his own behalf, and was entrusted by the best farmers in the Highlands in preference to any other drover in that district. He might have increased his business to any extent had he condescended to manage it by deputy; but except a lad or two, sister's sons of his own, Robin rejected the idea of assistance, conscious, perhaps, how much his reputation depended upon his attending in person to the practical discharge of his duty in every instance. He remained, therefore, contented with the highest premium given to persons of his description, and comforted himself with the hopes that a few journeys to England might enable him to conduct business on his own account, in a manner becoming his birth. For Robin Oig's father, Lachlan M'Combich(or *son of my friend,* his actual clan-surname being M'Gregor), had been so called by the celebrated Rob Roy, because of the particular friendship which had subsisted between the grandsire of Robin and that renowned cateran. Some people even say that Robin Oig derived his Christian name from one as renowned in the wilds of Loch Lomond as ever was his namesake Robin Hood, in the precincts of merry Sherwood. 'Of such ancestry,' as James Boswell says, 'who would not be proud?' Robin Oig was proud accordingly; but his frequent visits to England and to the Lowlands had given him tact enough to know that pretensions, which still gave him a little right to distinction in his own lonely glen, might be both obnoxious and ridiculous if preferred elsewhere. The pride of birth, therefore, was like the miser's treasure, the secret subject of his contemplation, but never exhibited to strangers as a subject of boasting.

Many were the words of gratulation and good luck which were bestowed on Robin Oig. The judges commended his drove, especially Robin's own property, which were the best of them. Some thrust out their snuff-mulls for the parting pinch—others tendered the *doch-an-dorrach* or parting cup. All cried—'Good luck travel with you and come home with you.—Give you luck in the Saxon market—brave notes in the *leabhar-dhu*' (black pocket-book) 'and plenty of English gold in the *sporran*(pouch of goatskin).

The bonny lasses made their adieus more modestly, and more than one, it was said would have given her best brooch to be certain that it was upon her that his eye last rested as he turned towards the road.

Robin Oig had just given the preliminary *'Hoo-hoo!'* to urge forward the loiterers of the drove, when there was a cry behind him.

'Stay, Robin—bide a blink. Here is Janet of Tomahourich —auld Janet, your father's sister.'

'Plague on her, for an auld Highland witch and spaewife,' said a farmer from the Carse of Stirling; 'she'll cast some of her cantrips on the cattle.'

'She canna do that,' said another sapient of the same profession—'Robin Oig is no the lad to leave any of them without tying St. Mungo's knot on their tails, and that will put to her speed the best witch that ever flew over Dimayet upon a broomstick.'

It may not be indifferent to the reader to know that the Highland cattle are peculiarly liable to be *taken,* or infected, by spells and witchcraft; which judicious people guard against by knitting knots of peculiar complexity on the tuft of hair which terminates the animal's tail.

But the old woman who was the object of the farmer's suspicion seemed only busied about the drover, without paying any attention to the drove. Robin, on the contrary, appeared rather impatient of her presence.

'What auld-world fancy,' he said, 'has brought you so early from the ingle-side this morning, Muhme? I am sure I bid you good-even, and had your God-speed, last night.'

'And left me more siller than the useless old woman will use till you come back again, bird of my bosom,' said the sibyl. 'But it is little I would care for the food that nourishes me, or the fire that warms me, or for God's blessed sun itself, if aught but weel should happen to the grandson of my father. So let me walk the *deasil* round you, that you may go safe out into the foreign land, and come safe home.'

Robin Oig stopped, half embarrassed, half laughing, and signing to those near that he only complied with the old woman to soothe her humour. In the meantime she traced around him, with wavering steps, the propitiation, which some have thought has been derived from the Druidical mythology. It consists, as is well known, in the person who makes the *deasil* walking three times round the person who is the object of the ceremony, taking care to move according to the course of the sun. At once, however, she stopped short, and exclaimed, in a voice of alarm and horror,

'Grandson of my father, there is blood on your hand.'

'Hush, for God's sake, aunt,' said Robin Oig; 'you will bring more trouble on yourself with this Taishataragh' (second sight) 'than you will be able to get out of for many a day.'

The old woman only repeated, with a ghastly look, 'There is blood on your hand, and it is English blood. The blood of the Gael is richer and redder. Let us see—let us——'

Ere Robin Oig could prevent her, which, indeed, could only have been done by positive violence, so hasty and peremptory were her proceedings, she had drawn from his side the dirk which lodged in the folds of his plaid, and held it up, exclaiming, although the weapon gleamed clear and bright in the sun, 'Blood, blood——Saxon blood again. Robin Oig M'Combich, go not this day to England!'

'Prutt, trutt,' answered Robin Oig, 'that will never do neither—it would be next thing to running the country. For shame, Muhme—give me the dirk. You cannot tell by the colour the difference betwixt the blood of a black bullock and a white one, and you speak of knowing Saxon from Gaelic blood. All men have their blood from Adam, Muhme. Give me my skene-dhu, and let me go on my road. I should have been half-way to Stirling Brig by this time.— Give me my dirk, and let me go.'

'Never will I give it to you,' said the old woman. 'Never will I quit my hold on your plaid, unless you promise me not to wear that unhappy weapon.'

The women around him urged him also, saying few of his aunt's words fell to the ground; and as the Lowland farmers continued to look moodily on the scene, Robin Oig determined to close it at any sacrifice.

'Well, then,' said the young drover, giving the scabbard of the weapon to Hugh Morrison, 'you Lowlanders care nothing for these freats. Keep my dirk for me. I cannot give it to you, because it was my father's; but your drove follows ours, and I am content it should be in your keeping, not in mine.—Will this do, Muhme?'

'It must,' said the old woman—'that is, if the Lowlander is mad enough to carry the knife.'

The strong westlandman laughed aloud.

'Goodwife,' said he, 'I am Hugh Morrison from Glenae, come of the Manly Morrisons of auld langsyne, that never took short weapon against a man in their lives. And neither needed they. They had their broadswords, and I have this bit supple,' showing a formidable cudgel—'for dirking ower the board, I leave that to John Highlandman.—Ye needna snort, none of you Highlanders, and you in especial, Robin. I'll keep the bit knife, if you are feared for the auld spaewife's tale, and give it back to you whenever you want it.'

Robin was not particularly pleased with some part of Hugh Morrison's speech; but he had learned in his travels more patience than belonged to his Highland constitution originally, and he accepted the service of the descendant of the Manly Morrisons without finding fault with the rather depreciating manner in which it was offered.

'If he had not had his morning in his head, and been but a Dumfriesshire hog into the boot, he would have spoken more like a gentleman. But you cannot have more of a sow than a grumph. It's shame my father's knife should ever slash a haggis for the like of him.'

Thus saying (but saying it in Gaelic)Robin drove on his cattle, and waved farewell to all behind him. He was in the greater haste, because he expected to join at Falkirk a comrade and brother in profession, with whom he proposed to travel in company.

Robin Oig's chosen friend was a young Englishman, Harry Wakefield by name, well known at every northern market, and in his way as much famed and honoured as our Highland driver of bullocks. He was nearly six feet high,

gallantly formed to keep the rounds at Smithfield, or
maintain the ring at a wrestling match; and although he
might have been overmatched, perhaps, among the regular
professors of the Fancy, yet, as a yokel, or rustic, or a chance
customer, he was able to give a bellyful to any amateur of
the pugilistic art. Doncaster races saw him in his glory,
betting his guinea, and generally successfully; nor was there
a main fought in Yorkshire, the feeders being persons of
celebrity, at which he was not to be seen, if business
permitted. But though a *sprack* lad, and fond of pleasure and
its haunts, Harry Wakefield was steady, and not the cautious
Robin Oig M'Combich himself was more attentive to the
main chance. His holidays were holidays indeed; but his
days of work were dedicated to steady and persevering
labour. In countenance and temper, Wakefield was the
model of old England's merry yeomen, whose clothyard
shafts, in so many hundred battles, asserted her superiority
over the nations, and whose good sabres in our own time
are her cheapest and most assured defence. His mirth was
readily excited; for, strong in limb and constitution, and
fortunate in circumstances, he was disposed to be pleased
with everything about him; and such difficulties as he might
occasionally encounter were, to a man of his energy, rather
matter of amusement than serious annoyance. With all the
merits of a sanguine temper, our young English drover was
not without his defects. He was irascible, sometimes to the
verge of being quarrelsome; and perhaps not the less
inclined to bring his disputes to a pugilistic decision,
because he found few antagonists able to stand up to him in
the boxing ring.

It is difficult to say how Harry Wakefield and Robin Oig
first became intimates; but it is certain a close acquaintance
had taken place betwixt them, although they had apparently
few common subjects of conversation or of interest, so soon
as their talk ceased to be of bullocks. Robin Oig, indeed,

spoke the English language rather imperfectly upon any other topics but stots and kyloes, and Harry Wakefield could never bring his broad Yorkshire tongue to utter a single word of Gaelic. It was in vain Robin spent a whole morning, during a walk over Minch Moor in attempting to teach his companion to utter, with true precision, the shibboleth *Llhu,* which is the Gaelic for calf. From Traquair to Murder-cairn, the hill rang with the discordant attempts of the Saxon upon the unmanageable monosyllable, and the heartfelt laugh which followed every failure. They had, however, better modes of awakening the echoes; for Wakefield could sing many a ditty to the praise of Moll, Susan, and Cicely, and Robin Oig had a particular gift at whistling interminable pibrochs through all their involutions, and what was more agreeable to his com-panion's southern ear, knew many of the northern airs, both lively and pathetic, to which Wakefield learned to pipe a bass. This, though Robin could hardly had comprehended his companion's stories about horse-racing, and cock-fighting or fox-hunting, and although his own legends of clan-fights and *creaghs,* varied with talk of Highland goblins and fairy folk, would have been caviare to his companion, they contrived nevertheless to find a degree of pleasure in each other's company, which had for three years back induced them to join company and travel together, when the direction of their journey permitted. Each, indeed, found his advantage in this companionship; for where could the Englishman have found a guide through the Western Highlands like Robin Oig M'Combich? and when they were on what Harry called the *right* side of the Border, his patronage, which was extensive, and his purse which was heavy, were at all times in the service of his Highland friend, and on many occasions his liberality did him genuine yeoman's service.

Were ever two such loving friends!—
How could they disagree?
O thus it was, he loved him dear,
And thought how to requite him,
And having no friend left but he,
He did resolve to fight him.

Duke upon Duke

The pair of friends had traversed with their usual cordiality the grassy wilds of Liddesdale, and crossed the opposite part of Cumberland, emphatically called The Waste. In these solitary regions, the cattle under the charge of our drovers derived their subsistence chiefly by picking their food as they went along the drove-road, or sometimes by the tempting opportunity of a *start and owerloup,* or invasion of the neighbouring pasture, where an occasion presented itself. But now the scene changed before them; they were descending towards a fertile and enclosed country, where no such liberties could be taken with impunity, or without a previous arrangement and bargain with the possessors of the ground. This was more especially the case, as a great northern fair was upon the eve of taking place, where both the Scotch and English drover expected to dispose of a part of their cattle, which it was desirable to produce in the market, rested and in good order. Fields were therefore difficult to be obtained, and only upon high terms. This necessity occasioned a temporary separation betwixt the two friends, who went to bargain, each as he could, for the separate accommodation of his herd. Unhappily it chanced that both of them, unknown to each other, thought of bargaining for the ground they wanted on the property of a country gentleman of some fortune, whose estate lay in the neighbourhood. The English drover applied to the bailiff on the property, who was known to him. It chanced that the Cumbrian squire, who had entertained some suspicions of his manager's honesty, was taking occasional measures to ascertain how far they were well founded, and had desired that any inquiries about his enclosures, with a view to occupy them for a temporary purpose, should be referred to himself. As, however, Mr. Ireby had gone the day before upon a journey of some miles' distance to the northward, the bailiff chose to consider the check upon his full powers as for the time removed, and concluded that he should best consult his master's interest, and perhaps his own, in making an agreement with Harry Wakefield. Meanwhile, ignorant of what his comrade was doing, Robin Oig, on his side, chanced to be overtaken by a good-looking smart little man upon a pony, most knowingly hogged and cropped, as was then the fashion, the rider wearing tight leather breeches and long-necked bright spurs. This cavalier asked one or two pertinent questions about markets and the price of stock. So Robin, seeing him a well-judging civil gentleman, took the freedom to ask him whether he could let him know if there was any grass-land to be let in that neighbourhood, for the temporary accommodation of his drove. He could not have put the question to more willing ears. The gentleman of the buckskin was the proprietor with whose bailiff Harry Wakefield had dealt or was in the act of dealing.

'Thou art in good luck, my canny Scot,' said Mr. Ireby, 'to have spoken to me, for I see thy cattle have done their day's work, and I have at my disposal the only field within three miles that is to be let in these parts.'

'The drove can pe gang two, three, four miles very pratty weel indeed,' said the cautious Highlander; 'put what would his honour be axing for the peasts pe the head, if she was to tak the park for twa or three days?'

'We won't differ, Sawney, if you let me have six stots for winterers, in the way of reason.'

'And which peasts wad your honour pe for having?'

'Why—let me see—the two black—the dun one—yon doddy—him with the twisted horn—the brockit—How much by the head?'

'Ah,' said Robin, 'your honour is a shudge—a real shudge —I couldna have set off the pest six peasts petter mysell, me that ken them as if they were my pairns, puir things.'

'Well, how much per head, Sawney?' continued Mr. Ireby.

'It was high markets at Doune and Falkirk,' answered Robin.

And thus the conversation proceeded, until they had agreed on the *prix juste* for the bullocks, the squire throwing in the temporary accommodation of the enclosure for the cattle into the boot, and Robin making, as he thought, a very good bargain, provided the grass was but tolerable. The squire walked his pony alongside of the drove, partly to show him the way, and see him put into possession of the field, and partly to learn the latest news of the northern markets.

They arrived at the field, and the pasture seemed excellent. But what was their surprise when they saw the bailiff quietly inducting the cattle of Harry Wakefield into the grassy Goshen which had just been assigned to those of Robin Oig M'Combich by the proprietor himself! Squire Ireby set spurs to his horse, dashed up to his servant, and learning what had passed between the parties, briefly informed the English drover that his bailiff had let the ground without his authority, and that he might seek grass for his cattle wherever he would, since he was to get none there. At the same time he rebuked his servant severely for having transgressed his commands, and ordered him instantly to assist in ejecting the hungry and weary cattle of Harry Wakefield, which were just beginning to enjoy a meal of unusual plenty, and to introduce those of his comrade, whom the English drover now began to consider as a rival.

The feelings which arose in Wakefield's mind would have induced him to resist Mr. Ireby's decision; but every Englishman has a tolerably accurate sense of law and justice, and John Fleecebumpkin, the bailiff, having acknowledged that he had exceeded his commission, Wakefield saw nothing else for it than to collect his hungry and disappointed charge and drive them on to seek quarters elsewhere. Robin Oig saw what had happened with regret, and hastened to offer to his English friend to share with him the disputed possession. But Wakefield's pride was severely hurt, and he answered disdainfully, 'Take it all, man—take it all—never make two bites of a cherry—thou canst talk over the gentry, and blear a plain man's eye—Out upon you, man—I would not kiss any man's dirty latchets for leave to bake in his oven.'

Robin Oig, sorry but not surprised at his comrade's displeasure, hastened to entreat his friend to wait but an hour 'till he had gone to the squire's house to receive payment for the cattle he had sold, and he could come back and help him to drive the cattle into some convenient place of rest, and explain to him the whole mistake they had both of them fallen into. But the Englishman continued indignant: 'Thou hast been selling, has thou? Ay, ay,—thou is a cunning lad for kenning the hours of bargaining. Go to the devil with thyself, for I will ne'er see thy fause loon's visage again—thou should be ashamed to look me in the face.'

'I am ashamed to look no man in the face,' said Robin Oig, something moved; 'and moreover I will look you in the face this blessed day, if you will bide at the clachan down younder.'

'Mayhap you had as well keep away,' said his comrade; and turning his back on his former friend, he collected his unwilling associates, assisted by the bailiff, who took some real and some affected interest in seeing Wakefield accommodated.

After spending some time in negotiating with more than one of the neighbouring farmers, who could not, or would not, afford the accommodation desired, Harry Wakefield at last, and in his necessity, accomplished his point by means of the landlord of the ale-house at which Robin Oig and he had agreed to pass the night, when they first separated from each other. Mine host was content to let him turn his cattle on a piece of barren moor, at a price little less than the bailiff had asked for the disputed enclosure; and the wretchedness of the pasture, as well as the price paid for it, were set down as exaggerations of the breach of faith and friendship of his Scottish crony. This turn of Wakefield's passions was encouraged by the bailiff (who had his own reasons for being offended against poor Robin, as having been the unwitting cause of his falling into disgrace with his master), as well as by the innkeeper, and two or three chance guests, who stimulated the drover in his resentment against his quondam associate,—some from the ancient grudge against the Scots which, when it exists anywhere, is to be found lurking in the Border counties, and some from the general love of mischief, which characterizes mankind in all ranks of life, to the honour of Adam's children be it spoken. Good John Barleycorn also, who always heightens and exaggerates the prevailing passions, be they angry or kindly, was not wanting in his offices on this occasion; and confusion to false friends and hard masters was pledged in more than one tankard.

In the meanwhile Mr. Ireby found some amusement in detaining the northern drover at his ancient hall. He caused a cold round of beef to be placed before the Scot in the butler's pantry, together with a foaming tankard of home-brewed, and took pleasure in seeing the hearty appetite with which these unwonted edibles were discussed by Robin Oig M'Combich. The squire himself lighting his pipe, compounded between his patrician dignity and his love of agricultural gossip, by walking up and down while he conversed with his guest.

'I passed another drove,' said the squire, 'with one of your countrymen behind them—they were something less beasts than your drove, doddies most of them—a big man was with them—none of your kilts though, but a decent pair of breeches—D'ye know who he may be?'

'Hout aye—that might, could, and would be Hughie Morrison—I didna think he could hae peen sae weel up. He has made a day on us; but his Argyleshires will have wearied shanks. How far was he pehind?'

'I think about six or seven miles,' answered the squire, 'for I passed them at the Christenbury Crag, and I overtook you at the Hollan Bush. If his beasts be leg-weary, he will maybe be selling bargains.'

'Na, na, Hughie Morrison is no the man for pargains—ye maun come to some Highland body like Robin Oig hersell for the like of these—put I maun pe wishing you goot night, and twenty of them let alane ane, and I maun down to the clachan to see if the lad Harry Waakfelt is out of his humdudgeons yet.'

The party at the alehouse was still in full talk, and the treachery of Robin Oig still the theme of conversation, when the supposed culprit entered the apartment. His arrival, as usually happens in such a case, put an instant stop to the discussion of which he had furnished the subject, and he was received by the company assembled with that chilling silence which, more than a thousand exclamations, tells an intruder that he is unwelcome. Surprised and offended, but not appalled by the reception which he experienced, Robin entered with an undaunted and even haughty air, attempted no greeting as he saw he was received with none, and placed himself by the side of the fire, a little apart from a table at which Harry Wakefield, the bailiff, and two or three other persons were seated. The ample Cumbrian kitchen would have afforded plenty of room, even for a larger separation.

Robin, thus seated, proceeded to light his pipe, and call for a pint of twopenny.

'We have no twopence ale,' answered Ralph Heskett, the landlord; 'but as thou findest thy own tobacco, it's like thou mayest find thy own liquor too—it's the wont of thy country, I wot.'

'Shame, goodman,' said the landlady, a blithe bustling housewife, hastening herself to supply the guest with liquor —'Thou knowest well enow what the strange man wants, and it's thy trade to be civil, man. Thou shouldst know, that if the Scot likes a small pot, he pays a sure penny.

Without taking any notice of this nuptial dialogue, the Highlander took the flagon in his hand, and addressing the company generally, drank the interesting toast of 'Good markets', to the party assembled.

'The better that the wind blew fewer dealers from the north,' said one of the farmers, 'and fewer Highland runts to eat up the English meadows.'

'Saul of my pody, put you are wrang there, my friend,' answered Robin, with composure, 'it is you fat Englishmen that eat up our Scots cattle, puir things.'

'I wish there was a summat to eat up their drovers,' said another; 'a plain Englishman canna make bread within a kenning of them.'

'Or an honest servant keep his master's favour, but they will come sliding in between him and the sunshine,' said the bailiff.

'If these pe jokes,' said Robin Oig, with the same composure, 'there is ower mony jokes upon one man.'

'It is no joke, but downright earnest,' said the bailiff. 'Harkye, Mr. Robin Ogg, or whatever is your name, it's right we should tell you that we are all of one opinion, and that is that you, Mr. Robin Ogg, have behaved to our friend, Mr. Harry Wakefield here, like a raff and a blackguard.'

'Nae doubt, nae doubt,' answered Robin, with great composure; 'and you are a set of very petty judges, for whose prains or pehaviour I wad not gie a pinch of sneeshing. If Mr. Harry Waakfelt kens where he is wranged, he kens where he may be righted.'

'He speaks truth,' said Wakefield, who had listened to what passed, divided between the offence which he had taken at Robin's late behaviour, and the revival of his habitual feelings of regard.

He now arose, and went towards Robin, who got up from his seat as he approached, and held out his hand.

'That's right, Harry—go it—serve him out,' resounded on all sides—'tip him the nailer—show him the mill.'

'Hold your peace all of you and be—,' said Wakefield; and then addressing his comrade, he took him by the extended hand, with something alike of respect and defiance. 'Robin,' he said, 'thou hast used me ill enough this day; but if you mean, like a frank fellow, to shake hands, and make a tussle for love on the sod, why I'll forgie thee, man, and we shall be better friends than ever.'

'And would it not pe petter to be cood friends without more of the matter?' said Robin; 'we will be much petter friendships with our panes hale than proken.'

Harry Wakefield dropped the hand of his friend, or rather threw it from him.

'I did not think I had been keeping company for three years with a coward.'

'Coward pelongs to none of my name,' said Robin, whose eyes began to kindle, but keeping the command of his temper. 'It was no coward's legs or hands, Harry Waakfelt, that drew you out of the fords of Frew, when you was drifting ower the plack rock, and every eel in the river expected his share of you.'

'And that is true enough, too,' said the Englishman, struck by the appeal.

'Adzooks!' exclaimed the bailiff—'sure Harry Wakefield, the nattiest lad at Whitson Tryste, Wooler Fair, Carlisle Sands, or Stagshaw Bank, is not going to show white feather? Ah, this comes of living so long with kilts and bonnets—men forget the use of their daddles.'

'I may teach you, Master Fleecebumpkin, that I have not lost the use of mine,' said Wakefield, and then went on. 'This will never do, Robin. We must have a turn-up, or we shall be the talk of the country-side. I'll be d——d if I hurt thee—I'll put on the gloves gin thou like. Come, stand forward like a man.'

'To pe peaten like a dog,' said Robin; 'is there any reason in that? If you think I have done you wrong, I'll go before your shudge, though I neither know his law nor his language.'

A general cry of 'No, no—no law, no lawyer! a bellyful and be friends,' was echoed by the bystanders.

'But,' continued Robin, 'if I am to fight, I've no skill to fight like a jackanapes, with hands and nails.'

'How would you fight, then?' said his antagonist; 'though I am thinking it would be hard to bring you to the scratch anyhow.'

'I would fight with proadswords, and sink point on the first plood drawn, like a gentleman.'

A loud shout of laughter followed the proposal, which indeed had rather escaped from poor Robin's swelling heart, than been the dictate of his sober judgement.

'Gentleman, quotha!' was echoed on all sides, with a shot of unextinguishable laughter; 'a very pretty gentleman, God wot—Canst get two swords for the gentlemen to fight with, Ralph Heskett?'

'No, but I can send to the armoury at Carlisle, and lend them two forks, to be making shift with in the meantime.'

'Tush, man,' said another, 'the bonny Scots come into the world with the blue bonnet on their heads, and dirk and pistol at their belt.'

'Best send post,' said Mr. Fleecebumpkin, 'to the squire of Corby Castle, to come and stand second to the *gentleman.*'

In the midst of this torrent of general ridicule, the Highlander instinctively griped beneath the folds of his plaid.

'But it's better not,' he said in his own language. 'A hundred curses on the swine-eaters, who know neither decency nor civility!'

'Make room, the pack of you,' he said, advancing to the door.

But his former friend interposed his sturdy bulk, and opposed his leaving the house; and when Robin Oig attempted to make his way by force, he hit him down on the floor, with as much ease as a boy bowls down a nine-pin.

'A ring, a ring!' was now shouted, until the dark rafters, and the hams that hung on them, trembled again, and the very platters on the *bink* clattered against each other. 'Well done, Harry'—'Give it him home, Harry'—'Take care of him now—he sees his own blood!'

Such were the exclamations, while the Highlander, starting from the ground, all his coldness and caution lost in frantic rage, sprang at his antagonist with the fury, the activity, and the vindictive purpose of an incensed tiger-cat. But when could rage encounter science and temper? Robin Oig again went down in the unequal contest; and as the blow was necessarily a severe one, he lay motionless on the floor of the kitchen. The landlady ran to offer some aid, but Mr. Fleecebumpkin would not permit her to approach.

'Let him alone,' he said, 'he will come to within time, and come up to scratch again. He has not got half his broth yet.'

'He has got all I mean to give him, though,' said his antagonist, whose heart began to relent towards his old associate; 'and I would rather by half give the rest to yourself, Mr. Fleecebumpkin, for you pretend to know a thing or two, and Robin had not art enough even to peel before setting to, but fought with his plaid dangling about him.—Stand up, Robin, my man! all friends now; and let me hear the man that will speak a word against you, or your country, for your sake.'

Robin Oig was still under the dominion of his passion, and eager to renew the onset; but being withheld on the one side by the peace-making Dame Heskett, and on the other, aware that Wakefield no longer meant to renew the combat, his fury sank into gloomy sullenness.

'Come, come, never grudge so much as it, man,' said the brave-spirited Englishman, with the placability of his country, 'shake hands, and we will be better friends than ever.'

'Friends!' exclaimed Robin Oig, with strong emphasis— 'friends!—Never. Look to yourself, Harry Waakfelt.'

'Then the curse of Cromwell on your proud Scots stomach, as the man says in the play, and you may do your worst, and be d——; for one man can say nothing more to another after a tussle, than that he is sorry for it.'

On these terms the friends parted; Robin Oig drew out, in silence, a piece of money, threw it on the table, and then left the alehouse. But turning at the door, he shook his hand at Wakefield, pointing with his forefinger upwards, in a manner which might imply either a threat or a caution. He then disappeared in the moonlight.

Some words passed after his departure between the bailiff, who piqued himself on being a little of a bully, and Harry Wakefield, who, with generous inconsistency, was now not indisposed to begin a new combat in defence of Robin Oig's reputation, 'although he could not use his daddles like an

Englishman, as it did not come natural to him.' But Dame Heskett prevented this second quarrel from coming to a head by her peremptory interference. 'There should be no more fighting in her house,' she said; 'there had been too much already.—And you, Mr. Wakefield, may live to learn,' she added,'what it is to make a deadly enemy out of a good friend.'

'Pshaw, dame! Robin Oig is an honest fellow, and will never keep malice.'

'Do not trust to that—you do not know the dour temper of the Scots, though you have dealt with them so often. I have a right to know them, my mother being a Scot.'

'And so is well seen on her daughter,' said Ralph Heskett.

This nuptial sarcasm gave the discourse another turn; fresh customers entered the tap-room or kitchen, and others left it. The conversation turned on the expected markets, and the report of prices from different parts both of Scotland and England—treaties were commenced, and Harry Wakefield was lucky enough to find a chap for a part of his drove, and at a very considerable profit; an event of consequence more than sufficient to blot out all remembrances of the unpleasant scuffle in the earlier part of the day. But there remained one party from whose mind that recollection could not have been wiped away by the possession of every head of cattle betwixt Esk and Eden.

This was Robin Oig M'Combich.—'That I should have had no weapon,' he said, 'and for the first time in my life!— Blighted by the tongue that bids the Highlander part with the dirk—the dirk—ha! the English blood!—My Muhme's word—when did her word fall to the ground?'

The recollection of the fatal prophecy confirmed the deadly intention which instantly sprang up in his mind.

'Ha! Morrison cannot be many miles behind; and if it were a hundred, what then?'

His impetuous spirit had now a fixed purpose and motive

of action, and he turned the light foot of his country towards the wilds, through which he knew, by Mr. Ireby's report, that Morrison was advancing. His mind was wholly engrossed by the sense of injury—injury sustained from a friend; and by the desire of vengeance on one whom he now accounted his most bitter enemy. The treasured ideas of self-importance and self-opinion—of ideal birth and quality, had become more precious to him (like the hoard to the miser) because he could only enjoy them in secret. But that hoard was pillaged, the idols which he had secretly worshipped had been desecrated and profaned. Insulted, abused, and beaten, he was no longer worthy, in his own opinion, of the name he bore or the lineage which he belonged to—nothing was left to him—nothing but revenge; and, as the reflection added a galling spur to every step, he determined it should be as sudden and signal as the offence.

When Robin Oig left the door of the alehouse, seven or eight English miles at least lay betwixt Morrison and him. The advance of the former was slow, limited by the sluggish pace of his cattle; the last left behind him stubble-field and hedge-row, crag and dark heath, all glittering with frost-rime in the broad November moonlight, at the rates of six miles an hour. And now the distant lowing of Morrison's cattle is heard; and now they are seen creeping like moles in size and slowness of motion on the broad face of the moor; and now he meets them—passes them, and stops their conductor.

'May good betide us,' said the Southlander. 'Is this you, Robin M'Combich, or your wraith?'

'It is Robin Oig M'Combich,' answered the Highlander, 'and it is not.—But never mind that, put pe giving me the skene-dhu.'

'What! you are for back to the Highlands—The devil!—Have you selt all of before the fair? This beats all for quick markets!'

'I have not sold—I am not going north—May pe I will never go north again.—Give me pack my dirk, Hugh Morrison, or there will pe words petween us.'

'Indeed, Robin, I'll be better advised before I gie it back to you—it is a wanchancy weapon in a Highlandman's hand, and I am thinking you will be about some barns-breaking.'

'Prutt, trutt! let me have my weapon,' said Robin Oig, impatiently.

'Hooly, and fairly,' said his well-meaning friend. 'I'll tell you what will do better than these dirking doings—Ye ken Highlander, and Lowlander, and Border-men, are a' ae man's bairns when you are over the Scots dyke. See, the Eskdale callants, and fighting Charlie of Liddesdale, and the Lockerby lads, and the four Dandies of Lustruther, and a wheen mair grey plaids, are coming up behind, and if you are wranged, there is the hand of a Manly Morrison, we'll see you righted, if Carlisle and Stanwix baith took up the feud.'

'To tell you the truth,' said Robin Oig, desirous of eluding the suspicions of his friend, 'I have enlisted with a party of the Black Watch, and must march off to-morrow morning.'

'Enlisted! Were you mad or drunk?—You must buy yourself off—I can lend you twenty notes, and twenty to that, if the drove sell.'

'I thank you—thank ye, Hughie; but I go with good will the gate that I am going,—so the dirk—the dirk!'

'There it is for you then, since less wunna serve. But think on what I was saying.—Waes me, it will be sair news in the braes of Balquidder, that Robin Oig M'Combich should have run an ill gate, and ta'en on.'

'Ill news in Balquidder, indeed!' echoed poor Robin. But Cot speed you, Hughie, and send you good marcats. Ye winna meet with Robin Oig again, either at tryste or fair.'

So saying, he shook hastily the hand of his acquaintance, and set out in the direction from which he had advanced, with the spirit of his former pace.

'There is something wrang with the lad,' muttered the Morrison to himself, 'but we'll maybe see better into the morn's morning.'

But long ere the morning dawned, the catastrophe of our tale had taken place. It was two hours after the affray had happened, and it was totally forgotten by almost every one, when Robin Oig returned to Heskett's inn. The place was filled at once by various sorts of men, and with noises corresponding to their character. There were the grave low sounds of men engaged in busy traffic, with the laugh, the song, and the riotous jest of those who had nothing to do but enjoy themselves. Among the last was Harry Wakefield, who, amidst a grinning group of smock-frocks, hobnailed shoes, and jolly English physiognomies, was trolling forth the old ditty,

> *What though my name be Roger,*
> *Who drives the plough and cart . . .*

when he was interrupted by a well-known voice saying in a high and stern tone, marked by the sharp Highland accent, 'Harry Waakfelt—if you be a man, stand up!'

'What is the matter?—what is it?' the guests demanded of each other.

'It is only a d——d Scotsman,' said Fleecebumpkin, who was by this time very drunk, 'whom Harry Wakefield helped to his broth the day, who is now come to have his *cauld kail* het again.'

'Harry Waakfelt,' repeated the same ominous summons, 'stand up, if you be a man!'

There is something in the tone of deep and concentrated passion, which attracts attention and imposes awe, even by the very sound. The guests shrank back on every side, and gazed at the Highlander as he stood in the middle of them, his brows bent, and his features rigid with resolution.

'I will stand up with all my heart, Robin, my boy, but it shall be to shake hands with you, and drink down all unkindness. It is not the fault of your heart, man, that you don't know how to clench your hands.'

But this time he stood opposite to his antagonist; his open and unsuspecting look strangely contrasted with the stern purpose, which gleamed wild, dark, and vindictive in the eyes of the Highlander.

' 'Tis not thy fault, man, that not having the luck to be an Englishman, thou canst not fight more than a schoolgirl.'

'I *can* fight,' answered Robin Oig sternly, but calmly, 'and you shall know it. You, Harry Waakfelt, showed me to-day how the Saxon churls fight—I show you now how the Highland Dunnièwassel fights.'

He seconded the word with the action, and plunged the dagger, which he suddenly displayed, into the broad chest of the English yeoman, with such fatal certainty and force, that the hilt made a hollow sound against the breast-bone, and the double-edged point split the very heart of his victim. Harry Wakefield fell and expired with a single groan. His assassin next seized the bailiff by the collar, and offered the blood poniard to his throat, whilst dread and surprise rendered the man incapable of defence.

'It were very just to lay you beside him,' he said, 'but the blood of a base pick-thank shall never mix on my father's dirk with that of a brave man.'

As he spoke, he cast the man from him with so much force that he fell on the floor, while Robin, with his other hand, threw the fatal weapon into the blazing turf-fire.

'There,' he said, 'take me who likes—and let fire cleanse blood if it can.'

The pause of astonishment still continuing, Robin Oig

asked for a peace-officer, and a constable having stepped out, he surrendered himself to his custody.

'A bloody night's work you have made of it,' said the constable.

'Your own fault,' said the Highlander. 'Had you kept his hands off me twa hours since, he would have been now as well and merry as he was twa minutes since.'

'It must be sorely answered,' said the peace-officer.

'Never mind that—death pays all debts; it will pay that too.'

The horror of the bystanders began now to give way to indignation; and the sight of a favourite companion murdered in the midst of them, the provocation being, in their opinion, so utterly inadequate to the excess of vengeance, might have induced them to kill the perpetrator of the deed upon the spot. The constable, however, did his duty on this occasion, and with the assistance of some of the more reasonable persons present, procured horses to guard the prisoner to Carlisle, to abide his doom at the next assizes. While the escort was preparing, the prisoner neither expressed the least interest nor attempted the slightest reply. Only, before he was carried from the fatal apartment, he desired to look at the dead body, which, raised from the floor, had been deposited upon the large table (at the head of which Harry Wakefield had presided but a few minutes before, full of life, vigour, and animation) until the surgeons should examine the mortal wound. The face of the corpse was decently covered with a napkin. To the surprise and horror of the bystanders, which displayed itself in a general *Ah!* drawn through clenched teeth and half-shut lips, Robin Oig removed the cloth, and gazed with a mournful but steady eye on the lifeless visage, which had been so lately animated that the smile of good-humoured confidence in his own strength, of conciliation at once and contempt towards his enemy, still curled his lip. While those present expected that the wound, which had so lately flooded the apartment with gore, would send forth fresh streams at the touch of the homicide, Robin Oig replaced the covering with the brief exclamation—'He was a pretty man!'

My story is nearly ended. The unfortunate Highlander stood his trial at Carlisle. I was myself present, and as a young Scottish lawyer, or barrister at least, and reputed a man of some quality, the politeness of the Sheriff of Cumberland offered me a place on the bench. The facts of the case were proved in the manner I have related them; and whatever might be at first the prejudice of the audience against a crime so un-English as that of assassination from revenge, yet when the rooted national prejudices of the prisoner had been explained, which made him consider himself as stained with indelible dishonour when subjected to personal violence; when his previous patience, moderation, and endurance were considered, the generosity of the English audience was inclined to regard his crime as the wayward aberration of a false idea of honour rather than as flowing from a heart naturally savage, or perverted by habitual vice. I shall never forget the charge of the venerable judge to the jury, although not at that time liable to be much affected either by that which was eloquent or pathetic.

'We have had,' he said, 'in the previous part of our duty' (alluding to some former trials) 'to discuss crimes which infer disgust and abhorrence, while they call down the well-merited vengeance of the law. It is now our still more melancholy task to apply its salutary though severe enactments to a case of a very singular character, in which the crime (for a crime it is, and a deep one) arose less out of the malevolence of the heart, than the error of the understanding—less from an idea of committing wrong, than from an unhappily perverted notion of that which is right. Here we have two men, highly esteemed, it has been stated, in their rank of life, and attached, it seems, to each other as friends, one of whose lives has been already sacrificed to a punctilio, and the other is about to prove the vengeance of the offended law; and yet both may claim our commiseration at least, as men acting in ignorance of each other's national prejudices, and unhappily misguided rather than voluntarily erring from the path of right conduct.

'In the original cause of the misunderstanding, we must in justice give the right to the prisoner at the bar. He had acquired possession of the enclosure, which was the object of competition, by a legal contract with the proprietor, Mr. Ireby; and yet, when accosted with reproaches undeserved in themselves, and galling doubtless to a temper at least sufficiently susceptible of passion, he offered notwithstanding to yield up half his acquisition for the sake of peace and good neighbourhood, and his amicable proposal was rejected with scorn. Then follows the scene at Mr. Heskett the publican's, and you will observe how the stranger was treated by the deceased, and, I am sorry to observe, by those around, who seem to have urged him in a manner which was aggravating in the highest degree. While he asked for peace and composition, and offered submission to a magistrate, or to a mutual arbiter, the prisoner was insulted by a whole company, who seem on this occasion to have forgotten the national maxim of "fair play"; and while attempting to escape from the place in peace, he was intercepted, struck down, and beaten to the effusion of his blood.

'Gentlemen of the jury, it was with some impatience that I heard my learned brother, who opened the case for the crown, give an unfavourable turn to the prisoner's conduct on this occasion. He said the prisoner was afraid to encounter his antagonist in fair fight, or to submit to the laws of the ring; and that therefore, like a cowardly Italian, he had recourse to his fatal stiletto, to murder the man whom he dared not meet in manly encounter. I observed the prisoner shrink from this part of the accusation with the abhorrence natural to a brave man; and as I would wish to make my words impressive when I point his real crime, I must secure his opinion of my impartiality, by rebutting everything that seems to me a false accusation. There can be no doubt that the prisoner is a man of resolution—too much resolution—I wish to Heaven that he had less, or rather that he had had a better education to regulate it.

'Gentlemen, as to the laws my brother talks of, they may be known in the bull-ring, or the bear-garden, or the cockpit, but they are not known here. Or, if they should be so far admitted as furnishing a species of proof that no malice was intended in this sort of combat, from which fatal accidents do sometimes arise, it can only be so admitted when both parties are *in pari casu,* equally acquainted with, and equally willing to refer themselves to, that species of arbitrament. But will it be contended that a man of superior rank and education is to be subjected, or is obliged to subject himself, to this coarse and brutal strife, perhaps in opposition to a younger, stronger, or more skilful opponent? Certainly even the pugilistic code, if founded upon the fair play of Merry Old England, as my brother alleges it to be, can contain nothing so preposterous. And, gentlemen of the jury, if the laws would support an English gentleman, wearing, we will suppose, his sword, in defending himself by force against a violent personal aggression of the nature offered to this prisoner, they will not less protect a foreigner and a stranger, involved in the same unpleasing circumstances. If, therefore, gentlemen of the jury, when thus pressed by a *vis major,* the object of obloquy to a whole company, and of direct violence from one at least, and, as he might reasonably apprehend, from more, the panel had produced the weapon which his countrymen, as we are informed, generally carry about their persons, and the same unhappy circumstance had ensued which you have heard detailed in evidence, I could not in my conscience have asked from you a verdict of murder. The prisoner's personal defence might, indeed, even in that case, have gone more or less beyond the *Moderamen inculpatae tutelae,* spoken of by lawyers, but the punishment incurred would have been that of manslaughter, not of murder. I beg leave to add that I should have thought this milder species of charge was demanded in the case supposed, notwithstanding the statute of James 1 cap. 8, which takes the case of slaughter by stabbing with a short weapon, even without malice prepense, out of the benefit of clergy. For this statute of stabbing, as it is termed, arose out of a temporary cause; and as the real guilt is the same, whether the slaughter be committed by the dagger, or the sword or pistol, the benignity of the modern law places them all on the same, or nearly the same footing.

'But, gentlemen of the jury, the pinch of the case lies in the interval of two hours interposed betwixt the reception of the injury and the fatal retaliation. In the heat of affray and *chaude mêlée,* law, compassionating the infirmities of humanity, makes allowance for the passions which rule such a stormy moment—for the sense of present pain, for the apprehension of further injury, for the difficulty of ascertaining with due accuracy the precise degree of violence which is necessary to protect the person of the individual, without annoying or injuring the assailant more than is absolutely requisite. But the time necessary to walk twelve miles, however speedily performed, was an interval sufficient for the prisoner to have recollected himself; and the violence with so many circumstances of deliberate determination, could neither be induced by the passion of anger, nor that of fear. It was the purpose and the act of predetermined revenge, for which law neither can, will, nor ought to have sympathy or allowance.

'It is true, we may repeat to ourselves, in alleviation of this poor man's unhappy action, that his case is a very peculiar one. The country which he inhabits was, in the days of many now alive, inaccessible to the laws, not only of England, which have not even yet penetrated thither, but to those to which our neighbours of Scotland are subjected, and which must be supposed to be, and no doubt actually are, founded upon the general principles of justice and equity which pervade every civilized country. Amongst their mountains, as among the North American Indians, the various tribes were wont to make war upon each other, so that each man was obliged to go armed for his protection. These men, from the ideas which they entertained of their own descent and of their own consequence, regarded them-selves as so many cavaliers or men-at-arms, rather than as the peasantry of a peaceful country. Those laws of the ring, as my brother terms them, were unknown to the race of warlike mountaineers; that decision of quarrels by no other weapons than those which nature has given every man, must to them have seemed as vulgar and as preposterous as to the noblesse of France. Revenge, on the other hand, must have been as familiar to their habits of society as to those of the Cherokees or Mohawks. It is indeed, as described by Bacon, at bottom a kind of wild untutored justice; for the fear of retaliation must withhold the hands of the oppressor where there is no regular law to check daring violence. But though all this may be granted, and though we may allow that, such having been the case of the Highlands in the days of the prisoner's fathers, many of the opinions and sentiments must still continue to influence the present generation, it cannot, and ought not, even in this most painful case, to alter the administration of the law, either in your hands, gentlemen of the jury, or in mine. The first object of civiliz-ation is to place the general protection of the law, equally administered, in the room of that wild justice, which every man cut and carved for himself, according to the length of his sword and the strength of his arm. The law says to the subjects, with a voice only inferior to that of the Deity, 'Vengeance is mine.' The instant that there is time for passion to cool, and reason to interpose, an injured party must become aware that the law assumes the exclusive cognizance of the right and wrong betwixt the parties, and opposes her inviolable buckler to every attempt of the private party to right himself. I repeat, that this unhappy man ought personally to be the object rather of our pity than our abhorrence, for he failed in his ignorance, and from mistaken notions of honour. But his crime is not the less that of murder, gentlemen, and, in your high and important office, it is your duty so to find. Englishmen have their angry passions as well as Scots; and should this man's action remain unpunished, you may unsheath, under various pretences, a thousand daggers betwixt the Land's-end and the Orkneys.'

The venerable judge thus ended what, to judge by his apparent emotion, and by the tears which filled his eyes, was really a painful task. The jury, according to his instructions, brought in a verdict of Guilty; and Robin Oig M'Combich, *alias* M'Gregor, was sentenced to death and left for execution, which took place accordingly. He met his fate with great firmness, and acknowledged the justice of his sentence. But he repelled indignantly the observations of those who accused him of attacking an unarmed man. 'I give a life for the life I took' he said, 'and what can I do more?'

from *Chronicles of the Canongate* 1827

THE HIGHLAND
WIDOW

THE HIGHLAND WIDOW

Chapter 1

It wound as near as near could be,
But what it is she cannot tell;
On the other side it seemed to be,
Of the huge broad-breasted old oak-tree.

                    Coleridge

M RS. Bethune Baliol's Memorandum begins thus:–
It is five-and-thirty, or perhaps nearer forty years
ago, since, to relieve the dejection of spirits occasioned by a
great family loss sustained two or three months before, I
undertook what was called the short Highland tour. This
had become in some degree fashionable; but though the
military roads were excellent, yet the accommodation was so
indifferent that it was reckoned a little adventure to
accomplish it. Besides, the Highlands, though now as
peaceable as any part of King George's dominions, was a
sound which still carried terror, while so many survived who
had witnessed the insurrection of 1745; and a vague idea of
fear was impressed on many, as they looked down from the
towers of Stirling northward to the huge chain of mountains
which rises like a dusky rampart to conceal in its recesses a
people whose dress, manners, and language differed still
very much from those of their lowland countrymen. For my
part, I come of a race not greatly subject to apprehensions
arising from imagination only. I had some Highland

relatives, knew several of their families of distinction; and, though only having the company of my bower-maiden, Mrs. Alice Lambskin, I went on my journey fearless.

But then I had a guide and cicerone almost equal to Greatheart in 'The Pilgrim's Progress,' in no less a person than Donald MacLeish, the postillion whom I hired at Stirling, with a pair of able-bodied horses, as steady as Donald himself, to drag my carriage, my duenna, and myself, wheresoever it was my pleasure to go.

Donald MacLeish was one of a race of post-boys whom, I suppose, mail-coaches and steam-boats have put out of fashion. They were to be found chiefly at Perth, Stirling, or Glasgow, where they and their horses were usually hired by travellers, or tourists, to accomplish such journeys of business or pleasure as they might have to perform in the land of the Gael. This class of persons approached to the character of what is called abroad a *conducteur;* or might be compared to the sailing-master on board a British ship of war, who follows out after his own manner the course which the captain commands him to observe. You explained to your postillion the length of your tour, and the objects you were desirous it should embrace; and you found him perfectly competent to fix the places of rest or refreshment, with due attention that those should be chosen with reference to your convenience, and to any points of interest which you might desire to visit.

The qualifications of such a person were necessarily much superior to those of the 'first ready,' who gallops thrice a day over the same ten miles. Donald MacLeish, besides being quite alert at repairing all ordinary accidents to his horses and carriage, and in making shift to support them, where forage was scarce, with such substitutes as bannocks and cakes, was likewise a man of intellectual resources. He had acquired a general knowledge of the traditional stories of the country which he had traversed so often; and, if encouraged (for Donald was a man of the most decorous reserve), he would willingly point out to you the site of the principal clan-battles, and recount the most remarkable legends by which the road, and the objects which occurred in travelling it, had been distinguished. There was some originality in the man's habits of thinking and expressing himself, his turn for legendary lore strangely contrasting with a portion of the knowing shrewdness belonging to his actual occupation, which made his conversation amuse the way well enough.

Add to this, Donald knew all his peculiar duties in the country which he traversed so frequently. He could tell, to a day, when they would 'be killing' lamb at Tyndrum or Glenuilt; so that the stranger would have some chance of being fed like a christian; and knew to a mile the last village where it was possible to procure a wheaten loaf, for the guidance of those who were little familiar with the Land of Cakes. He was acquainted with the road every mile, and could tell to an inch which side of a Highland bridge was passable, which decidedly dangerous. In short, Donald MacLeish was not only our faithful attendant and steady servant, but our humble and obliging friend; and though I have known the half-classical cicerone of Italy, the talkative French *valet de place,* and even the muleteer of Spain, who piques himself on being a maize-eater, and whose honour is not to be questioned without danger, I do not think I have ever had so sensible and intelligent a guide.

Our motions were of course under Donald's direction; and it frequently happened, when the weather was serene, that we preferred halting to rest his horses even where there was no established stage, and taking our refreshment under a crag, from which leaped a waterfall, or beside the verge of a fountain enamelled with verdant turf and wild-flowers. Donald had an eye for such spots, and though he had, I dare say, never read 'Gil Blas' or 'Don Quixote,' yet he chose such halting-places as Le Sage or Cervantes would have described. Very often, as he observed the pleasure I took in conversing with the country people, he would manage to fix our place of rest near a cottage where there was some old Gael whose broadsword had blazed at Falkirk or Preston, and who seemed the frail yet faithful record of times which had passed away. Or he would contrive to quarter us, as far as a cup of tea went, upon the hospitality of some parish minister of worth and intelligence, or some country family of the better class, who mingled with the wild simplicity of their original manners, and their ready and hospitable welcome, a sort of courtesy belonging to a people the lowest of whom are accustomed to consider themselves as being, according to the Spanish phrase, 'as good gentlemen as the king, only not quite so rich.'

To all such persons Donald MacLeish was well known, and his introduction passed as current as if we had brought letters from some high chief of the country.

Sometimes it happened that the Highland hospitality which welcomed us with all the variety of mountain fare, preparations of milk and eggs, and girdle-cakes of various kinds, as well as more substantial dainties, according to the inhabitant's means of regaling the passenger, descended rather too exuberantly on Donald MacLeish in the shape of mountain dew. Poor Donald! he was on such occasions like Gideon's fleece, moist with the noble element, which, of course, fell not on us. But it was his only fault, and when pressed to drink *doch-an-dorroch* to my ladyship's good health, it would have been ill taken to have refused the pledge, nor was he willing to do such discourtesy. It was, I repeat, his only fault, nor had we any great right to complain; for if it rendered him a little more talkative, it augmented his ordinary share of punctilious civility, and he only drove slower and talked longer and more pompously than when he had not come by a drop of usquebaugh. It was, we remarked, only on such occasions that Donald talked with an air of importance of the family of MacLeish; and we had no title to be scrupulous in censuring a foible the consequences of which were confined within such innocent limits.

We became so much accustomed to Donald's mode of managing us, that we observed with some interest the art which he used to produce a little agreeable surprise, by concealing from us the spot where he proposed our halt to be made, when it was of an unusual and interesting character. This was so much his wont, that when he made apologies at setting off for being obliged to stop in some strange solitary place, till the horses should eat the corn which he brought on with them for that purpose, our imagination used to be on the stretch to guess what romantic retreat he had secretly fixed upon for our noontide baiting-place.

We had spent the great part of the morning at the delightful village of Dalmally, and had gone upon the lake under the guidance of the excellent clergyman who was then incumbent at Glenorchy, and had heard a hundred legends of the stern chiefs of Loch Awe, Duncan with the thrum bonnet, and the other lords of the now mouldering towers of Kilchurn. Thus it was later than usual when we set out on our journey, after a hint or two from Donald concerning the length of the way to the next stage, as there was no good halting-place between Dalmally and Oban.

Having bid adieu to our venerable and kind cicerone, we proceeded on our tour, winding round the tremendous mountain called Cruachan Ben, which rushes down in all its majesty of rocks and wilderness on the lake, leaving only a pass, in which, notwithstanding its extreme strength, the warlike clan of MacDougal of Lorn were almost destroyed by the sagacious Robert Bruce. That king, the Wellington of his day, had accomplished, by a forced march, the unexpected manoeuvre of forcing a body of troops round the other side of the mountain, and thus placed them in the flank and in the rear of the men of Lorn, whom at the same time he attacked in front. The great number of cairns yet visible, as you descend the pass on the westward side, shows the extent of the vengeance which Bruce exhausted on his inveterate and personal enemies. I am, you know, the sister of soldiers, and it has since struck me forcibly that the manoeuvre which Donald described resembled those of Wellington or of Bonaparte. He was a great man, Robert Bruce, even a Baliol must admit that; although it begins now to be allowed that his title to the crown was scarce so good as that of the unfortunate family with whom he contended—But let that pass.—The slaughter had been the greater, as the deep and rapid river Awe is disgorged from the lake, just in the rear of the fugitives, and encircles the base of the tremendous mountain; so that the retreat of the unfortunate fliers was intercepted on all sides by the inaccessible character of the country, which had seemed to promise them defence and protection.

Musing, like the Irish lady in the song, 'upon things which are long enough a-gone, we felt no impatience at the slow and almost creeping pace with which our conductor proceeded along General Wade's military road, which never or rarely condescends to turn aside from the steepest ascent, but proceeds right up and down hill, with the indifference to height and hollow, steep or level, indicated by the old Roman engineers. Still, however, the substantial excellence of these great works—for such are the military highways in the Highlands—deserved the compliment of the poet, who, whether he came from our sister kingdom, and spoke in his own dialect, or whether he supposed those whom he addressed might have some national pretension to the second sight, produced the celebrated couplet—

Had you but seen these roads *before* they were made,
You would hold up your hands, and bless General
   Wade.

Nothing indeed can be more wonderful than to see these
wildernesses penetrated and pervious in every quarter by
broad accesses of the best possible construction, and so
superior to what the country could have demanded for
many centuries for any pacific purpose of commercial intercourse. Thus the traces of war are sometimes happily
accommodated to the purposes of peace. The victories of
Bonaparte have been without results; but his road over the
Simplon will long be the communication betwixt peaceful
countries, who will apply to the ends of commerce and
friendly intercourse that gigantic work which was formed for
the ambitious purpose of warlike invasion.

   While we were thus stealing along, we gradually turned
round the shoulder of Ben Cruachan, and, descending the
course of the foaming and rapid Awe, left behind us the
expanse of the majestic lake which gives birth to that
impetuous river. The rocks and precipices which stooped
down perpendicularly on our path on the right hand
exhibited a few remains of the wood which once clothed
them, but which had in latter times been felled to supply,
Donald MacLeish informed us, the iron-foundries at the
Bunawe. This made us fix our eyes with interest on one large
oak, which grew on the left hand towards the river. It
seemed a tree of extraordinary magnitude and picturesque
beauty, and stood just where there appeared to be a few
roods of open ground lying among huge stones, which had
rolled down from the mountain. To add to the romance of
the situation, the spot of clear ground extended round the
foot of a proud-browed rock, from the summit of which
leaped a mountain stream in a fall of sixty feet, in which it
was dissolved into foam and dew. At the bottom of the fall

the rivulet with difficulty collected, like a routed general, its dispersed forces, and, as if tamed by its descent, found a noiseless passage through the heath to join the Awe.

I was much struck with the tree and waterfall, and wished myself nearer them; not that I thought of sketch-book or portfolio – for in my younger days misses were not accustomed to black-lead pencils, unless they could use them to some good purpose – but merely to indulge myself with a closer view. Donald immediately opened the chaise door, but observed it was rough walking down the brae, and that I would see the tree better by keeping the road for a hundred yards farther, when it passed closer to the spot for which he seemed, however, to have no predilection. 'He knew,' he said, 'a far bigger tree than that nearer Bunawe, and it was a place where there was flat ground for the carriage to stand, which it could simply do on these braes; – but just as my leddyship liked.'

My ladyship did choose rather to look at the fine tree before me than to pass it by in hopes of a finer; so we walked beside the carriage till we should come to a point from which, Donald assured us, we might, without scrambling, go as near the tree as we chose, 'though he wadna advise us to go nearer than the high-road.'

There was something grave and mysterious in Donald's sun-browned countenance when he gave us this intimation, and his manner was so different from his usual frankness, that my female curiosity was set in motion. We walked on the whilst, and I found the tree, of which we had now lost sight by the intervention of some rising ground, was really more distant than I had at first supposed. 'I could have sworn now,' said I to my cicerone, 'that yon tree and waterfall was the very place where you intended to make a stop to-day.'

'The Lord forbid!' said Donald hastily.

'And for what, Donald? Why should you be willing to pass so pleasant a spot?'

'It's ower near Dalmally, my leddy, to corn the beasts –
it would bring their dinner ower near their breakfast, poor
things:- an', besides, the place is not canny.'

'Oh! then the mystery is out. There is a bogle or a
brownie, a witch or gyrecarlin, a bodach or a fairy, in the
case?'

'The ne'er a bit, my leddy – ye are clean aff the road, as
I may say, But if your leddyship will just hae patience, and
wait till we are by the place and out of the glen, I'll tell
ye all about it. There is no much luck in speaking of such
things in the place they chanced in.'

I was obliged to suspend my curiosity, observing that, if
I persisted in twisting the discourse one way while Donald
was twining it another, I should make his objection,
like a hempen cord, just so much the tougher. At length
the promised turn of the road brought us within fifty paces
of the tree which I desired to admire, and I now saw, to my
surprise, that there was a human habitation among the cliffs
which surrounded it. It was a hut of the least dimensions
and most miserable description that I ever saw even in the
Highlands. The walls of sod, or *divot,* as the Scotch call it,
were not four feet high – the roof was of turf, repaired with
reeds and sedges – the chimney was composed of clay,
bound round by straw ropes – and the whole walls, roof and
chimney, were alike covered with vegetation of house-leek,
rye-grass and moss common to decayed cottages formed of
such materials. There was not the slightest vestige of a kale-
yard, the usual accompaniment of the very worst huts; and
of living things we saw nothing, save a kid which was brow-
sing on the roof of the hut, and a goat, its mother, as some
distance, feeding betwixt the oak and the river Awe.

'What man,' I could not help exclaiming, 'can have
committed sin deep enough to deserve such a miserable
dwelling!'

'Sin enough,' said Donald MacLeish, with a half-suppressed groan; 'and God he knoweth misery enough too; – and it is no man's dwelling neither, but a woman's.'

'A woman's!' I repeated, 'and in so lonely a place – What sort of a woman can she be?'

'Come this way, my leddy, and you may judge that for yourself,' said Donald. And by advancing a few steps, and making a sharp turn to the left, we gained a sight of the side of the great broad-breasted oak, in the direction opposed to that in which we had hitherto seen it.

'If she keeps her old wont, she will be there at this hour of the day,' said Donald, but immediately became silent, and pointed with his finger, as one afraid of being over-heard. I looked, and beheld, not without some sense of awe, a female form seated by the stem of the oak, with her head drooping, her hands clasped, and a dark-coloured mantle drawn over her head, exactly as Judah is represented in the Surian medals as seated under her palm-tree. I was infected with the fear and reverence which my guide seemed to enter-tain towards this solitary being, nor did I think of advancing towards her to obtain a nearer view until I had cast an in-quiring look on Donald; to which he replied in a half-whisper – 'She has been a fearfu' bad woman, my leddy.'

'Mad woman, said you,' replied I, hearing him im-perfectly; 'then she is perhaps dangerous?'

'No – she is not mad,' replied Donald; 'for then it may be she would be happier than she is; though when she thinks on what she has done, and caused to be done, rather than yield up a hair-breadth of her ain wicked will, it is not likely she can be very well settled. But she neither is mad nor mis-chievous; and yet, my leddy, I think you had best not to go nearer to her.' And then, in a few hurried words, he made me acquainted with the story which I am now to tell more in detail. I heard the narrative with a mixture of horror and sympathy, which at once impelled me to approach the sufferer and speak to her the words of comfort, or rather of pity, and at the same time made me afraid to do so.

This indeed was the feeling with which she was regarded by the Highlanders in the neighbourhood, who looked upon Elspat MacTavish, or the Woman of the Tree, as they called her, as the Greeks considered those who were pursued by the Furies, and endured the mental torment consequent on great criminal actions. They regarded such unhappy beings as Orestes and Oedipus as being less the voluntary perpetrators of their crimes than as the passive instruments by which the terrible decrees of Destiny had been accomplished; and the fear with which they beheld them was not unmingled with veneration.

I also learned further from Donald MacLeish that there was some apprehension of ill luck attending those who had the boldness to approach too near or disturb the awful solitude of a being so unutterably miserable; that it was supposed that whosoever approached her must experience in some respect the contagion of her wretchedness.

It was therefore with some reluctance that Donald saw me prepare to obtain a nearer view of the sufferer, and that he himself followed to assist me in the descent down a very rough path. I believe his regard for me conquered some ominous feelings in his own breast, which connected his duty on this occasion with the presaging fear of lame horses, lost linch-pins, overturns, and other perilous chances of the postillion's life.

I am not sure if my own courage would have carried me close to Elspat, had he not followed. There was in her countenance the stern abstraction of hopeless and overpowering sorrow, mixed with the contending feelings of remorse, and of the pride which struggled to conceal it. She guessed, perhaps, that it was curiosity, arising out of her uncommon story, which induced me to intrude on her solitude – and she could not be pleased that a fate like hers had been the theme of a traveller's amusement. Yet the look with which

she regarded me was one of scorn instead of embarrassment. The opinion of the world and all its children could
not add or take an iota from her load of misery; and, save
from the half-smile that seemed to intimate the contempt
of a being rapt by the very intensity of her affliction above
the sphere of ordinary humanities, she seemed as indifferent
to my gaze as if she had been a dead corpse or a marble
stone.

Elspat was above the middle stature; her hair, now griz-
zled, was still profuse, and it had been of the most decided
black. So were her eyes, in which, contradicting the stern
and rigid features of her countenance, there shone the wild
and troubled light that indicates an unsettled mind. Her
hair was wrapped round a silver bodkin with some attention
to neatness, and her dark mantle was disposed around her
with a degree of taste, though the materials were of the most
ordinary sort.

After gazing on this victim of guilt and calamity till I was
ashamed to remain silent, though uncertain how I ought to
address her, I began to express my surprise at her choosing
such a desert and deplorable dwelling. She cut short these
expressions of sympathy by answering in a stern voice, without the least change of countenance or posture, 'Daughter
of the stranger, he has told you my story.' I was silenced
at once, and felt how little all earthly accommodation must
seem to the mind which had such subjects as hers for
rumination. Without again attempting to open the conversation, I took a piece of gold from my purse (for Donald
had intimated she lived on alms), expecting she would at
least stretch her hand to receive it. But she neither accepted
nor rejected the gift – she did not even seem to notice it,
though twenty times as valuable, probably, as was usually
offered. I was obliged to place it on her knee, saying involuntarily, as I did so, 'May God pardon you, and relieve
you!' I shall never forget the look which she cast up to

heaven, nor the tone in which she exclaimed in the very words of my old friend, John Home –

'My beautiful – my brave!'

It was the language of nature, and arose from the heart of the deprived mother, as it did from that gifted imaginative poet while furnishing with appropriate expressions the ideal grief of Lady Randolph.

Chapter 2.

> *Oh, I'm come to the Low Country,*
> *Och, Och, ohonochie,*
> *Without a penny in my pouch*
> *To buy a meal for me.*
> *I was the proudest of my clan,*
> *Long, long may I repine;*
> *And Donald was the bravest man,*
> *And Donald he was mine.*

Old Song.

Elspat had enjoyed happy days, though her age had sunk into hopeless and inconsolable sorrow and distress. She was once the beautiful and happy wife of Hamish MacTavish, for whom his strength and feats of prowess had gained the title of MacTavish Mhor. His life was turbulent and dangerous, his habits being of the old Highland stamp, which esteemed it shame to want anything that could be had for the taking. Those in the Lowland line who lay near him, and desired to enjoy their lives and property in quiet, were contented to pay him a small composition, in name of protection money, and comforted themselves with the old proverb that it was better to 'fleech the de'il than fight him.' Others, who accounted such composition dishonourable, were often surprised by MacTavish Mhor and his associates and followers, who usually inflicted an adequate penalty, either in person or property, or both. The creagh is yet remembered in which he swept one hundred and fifty cows from Monteith in one drove; and how he placed the Laird of Ballybught naked in a slough, for having threatened to send for a party of the Highland Watch to protect his property.

Whatever were occasionally the triumphs of this daring cateran, they were often exchanged for reverses; and his narrow escapes, rapid flights, and the ingenious stratagems with which he extricated himself from imminent danger, were no less remembered and admired than the exploits in which he had been successful. In weal or woe, through every species of fatigue, difficulty, and danger, Elspat was his faithful companion. She enjoyed with him the fits of occasional prosperity; and when adversity pressed them hard, her strength of mind, readiness of wit, and courageous endurance of danger and toil are said often to have stimulated the exertions of her husband.

Their morality was of the old Highland cast, faithful friends and fierce enemies: the Lowland herds and harvests they accounted their own, whenever they had the means of driving off the one or of seizing upon the other; nor did the least scruple on the right of property interfere on such occasions. Hamish Mhor argued like the old Cretan warrior:

> My sword, my spear, my shaggy shield,
>   They make me lord of all below;
> For he who dreads the lance to wield,
>   Before my shaggy shield must bow.
> His lands, his vineyards, must resign,
>   And all that cowards have is mine.

But these days of perilous though frequently successful depredation began to be abridged, after the failure of the expedition of Prince Charles Edward. MacTavish Mhor had not sat still on that occasion, and he was outlawed, both as a traitor to the State and as a robber and cateran. Garrisons were now settled in many places where a redcoat had never before been seen, and the Saxon war-drum resounded among the most hidden recesses of the Highland mountains. The fate of MacTavish became every day more inevitable; and it was the more difficult for him to make his exertions for defence or escape, that Elspat, amid his evil days, had increased his family with an infant child, which was a considerable incumbrance upon the necessary rapidity of their motions.

At length the fatal day arrived. In a strong pass on the skirts of Ben Cruachan, the celebrated MacTavish Mhor was surprised by a detachment of the Sidier Roy. His wife assisted him heroically, charging his piece from time to time; and, as they were in possession of a post that was nearly unassailable, he might have perhaps escaped if his ammunition had lasted. But at length his balls were expended, although it was not until he had fired off most of the silver buttons from his waistcoat, and the soldiers, no longer deterred by fear of the unerring marksman, who had slain three, and wounded more of their number, approached his stronghold, and, unable to take him alive, slew him, after a most desperate resistance.

All this Elspat witnessed and survived, for she had, in the child which relied on her for support, a motive for strength and exertion. In what manner she maintained herself it is not easy to say. Her only ostensible means of support were a flock of three or four goats, which she fed wherever she pleased on the mountain pastures, no one challenging the intrusion. In the general distress of the country, her ancient acquaintances had little to bestow; but what they could part with from their own necessities they willingly devoted to the relief of others. From Lowlanders she sometimes demanded tribute rather than requested alms. She had not forgotten she was the widow of MacTavish Mhor, or that the child who trotted by her knee might, such were her imaginations, emulate one day the fame of his father, and command the same influence which he had exerted without control. She associated so little with others, went so seldom and so unwillingly from the wildest recesses of the mountains, where she usually dwelt with her goats, that she was quite unconscious of the great change which had taken place in the country around her, the substitution of civil order for military violence, and the strength gained by the law and its adherents over those who were called in Gaelic song 'the stormy sons of the sword.' Her own diminished consequence and straitened circumstances she indeed felt, but for this the death of MacTavish Mhor was, in her apprehension, a sufficing reason; and she doubted not that she should rise to her former state of importance, when Hamish Bean (or Fair-haired James) should be able to wield the arms of his father. If, then, Elspat was repelled rudely when she demanded anything necessary for her wants, or the accommodation of her little flock, by a churlish farmer, her threats of vengeance, obscurely expressed, yet terrible in their tenor, used frequently to extort, through fear of her maledictions, the relief which was denied to her necessities; and the trembling goodwife who gave meal or money to the widow of MacTavish Mhor wished in her heart that the stern old carline had been burnt on the day her husband had his due.

Years thus ran on, and Hamish Bean grew up, not indeed to be of his father's size or strength, but to become an active, high-spirited, fair-haired youth, with a ruddy cheek, an eye like an eagle, and all the agility, if not all the strength, of his formidable father, upon whose history and achievements his mother dwelt, in order to form her son's mind to a similar course of adventures. But the young see the present state of this changeful world more keenly than the old. Much attached to his mother, and disposed to do all in his power for her support, Hamish yet perceived, when he mixed with the world, that the trade of the cateran was now alike dangerous and discreditable, and that if he were to emulate his father's prowess it must be in some other line of warfare more consonant to the opinions of the present day.

As the faculties of mind and body began to expand, he became more sensible of the precarious nature of his situation, of the erroneous views of his mother, and her ignorance respecting the changes of the society with which she mingled so little. In visiting friends and neighbours he became aware of the extremely reduced scale to which his parent was limited, and learned that she possessed little or nothing more than the absolute necessaries of life, and that these were sometimes on the point of failing. At times his success in fishing and the chase was able to add something to her subsistence; but he saw no regular means of contributing to her support, unless by stooping to servile labour, which, if he himself could have endured it, would, he knew, have been like a death's-wound to the pride of his mother.

Elspat, meanwhile, saw with surprise that Hamish Bean, although now tall and fit for the field, showed no disposition to enter on his father's scene of action. There was something of the mother at her heart which prevented her from urging him in plain terms to take the field as a cateran, for the fear occurred of the perils into which the trade must conduct him; and, when she would have spoken to him on the subject, it seemed to her heated imagination as if the ghost of her husband arose between them in his bloody tartans, and, laying his finger on his lips, appeared to prohibit the topic. Yet she wondered at what seemed his want of spirit, sighed as she saw him from day to day lounging about in the long-skirted Lowland coat which the legislature had imposed upon the Gael instead of their own romantic garb, and thought how much nearer he would have resembled her husband had he been clad in the belted plaid and short hose, with his polished arms gleaming at his side.

Besides these subjects for anxiety, Elspat had others arising from the engrossing impetuosity of her temper. Her love of MacTavish Mhor had been qualified by respect and sometimes even by fear; for the cateran was not the species of man who submits to female government; but over his son she had exerted, at first during childhood, and afterwards in early youth, an imperious authority, which gave her maternal love a character of jealousy. She could not bear, when Hamish, with advancing life, made repeated steps towards independence, absented himself from her cottage at such season and for such length of time as he chose, and seemed to consider, although maintaining towards her every possible degree of respect and kindness, that the control and responsibility of his actions rested on himself alone. This would have been of little consequence, could she have concealed her feelings within her own bosom; but the ardour and impatience of her passions made her frequently show her son that she conceived herself neglected and ill used. When he was absent for any length of time from her cottage, without giving intimation of his purpose, her resentment of his return used to be so unreasonable that it naturally suggested to a young man fond of independence, and desirous to amend his situation in the world, to leave her, even for the very purpose of enabling him to provide for the parent whose egotistical demands on his filial attention tended to confine him to a desert in which both were starving in hopeless and helpless indigence.

Upon one occasion, the son having been guilty of some independent excursion, by which the mother felt herself affronted and disobliged, she had been more than usually violent on his return, and awakened in Hamish a sense of displeasure, which clouded his brow and cheek. At length, as she persevered in her unreasonable resentment, his patience became exhausted, and taking his gun from the chimney corner, and muttering to himself the reply which his respect for his mother prevented him from speaking aloud, he was about to leave the hut which he had but barely entered.

'Hamish,' said his mother, 'are you again about to leave me?' But Hamish only replied by looking at and rubbing the lock of his gun.

'Ay, rub the lock of your gun,' said his parent, bitterly. 'I am glad you have courage enough to fire it, though it be but at a roe-deer.' Hamish started at this undeserved taunt, and cast a look of anger at her in reply. She saw that she had found the means of giving him pain.

'Yes,' she said, 'look fierce as you will at an old woman, and your mother; it would be long ere you bent your brow on the angry countenance of a bearded man.'

'Be silent, mother, or speak of what you understand,' said Hamish, much irritated, 'and that is of the distaff and the spindle.'

'And was it of spindle and distaff that I was thinking when I bore you away on my back through the fire of six of the Saxon soldiers, and you a wailing child? I tell you, Hamish, I know a hundredfold more of swords and guns than ever you will; and you will never learn so much of noble war by yourself as you have seen when you were wrapped up in my plaid.'

'You are determined at least to allow me no peace at home, mother; but this shall have an end,' said Hamish, as, resuming his purpose of leaving the hut, he rose and went towards the door.

'Stay, I command you,' said his mother; 'stay! or may the gun you carry be the means of your ruin—may the road you are going be the track of your funeral!'

'What makes you use such words, mother?' said the young man, turning a little back. 'They are not good, and good cannot come of them. Farewell just now, we are too angry to speak together—farewell; it will be long ere you see me again' And he departed, his mother, in the first burst of her impatience, showering after him her maledictions, and in the next invoking them on her own head, so that they might spare her son's. She passed that day and the next in all the vehemence of impotent and yet unrestrained passion, now entreating Heaven, and such powers as were familiar to her by rude tradition, to restore her dear son, 'the calf of her heart'; now in impatient resentment, meditating with what bitter terms she should rebuke his filial disobedience upon his return, and now studying the most tender language to attach him to the cottage, which, when her boy was present, she would not, in the rapture of her affection, have exchanged for the apartments of Taymouth Castle.

Two days passed, during which, neglecting even the slender means of supporting nature which her situation afforded, nothing but the strength of a frame accustomed to hardships and privations of every kind could have kept her in existence, notwithstanding the anguish of her mind prevented her being sensible of her personal weakness. Her dwelling, at this period, was the same cottage near which I had found her, but then more habitable by the exertions of Hamish, by whom it had been in a great measure built and repaired.

It was on the third day after her son had disappeared, as she sat at the door rocking herself, after the fashion of her countrywomen when in distress or in pain, that the then unwonted circumstance occurred of a passenger being seen on the high-road above the cottage. She cast but one glance at him—he was on horseback, so that it could not be Hamish, and Elspat cared not enough for any other being

on earth, to make her turn her eyes towards him a second
time. The stranger, however, paused opposite to her cottage,
and, dismounting from his pony, led it down the steep and
broken path which conducted to her door.

'God bless you, Elspat MacTavish!'—She looked at the
man as he addressed her in her native language, with the
displeased air of one whose reverie is interrupted; but the
traveller went on to say, 'I bring you tidings of your son
Hamish.' At once, from being the most uninteresting object,
in respect to Elspat, that could exist, the form of the stranger
became awful in her eyes, as that of a messenger descended
from Heaven, expressly to pronounce upon her death or
life. She started from her seat, and with hands convulsively
clasped together, and held up to heaven, eyes fixed on the
stranger's countenance, and person stooping forward to
him, she looked those inquiries which her faltering tongue
could not articulate. 'Your son sends you his dutiful remembrance, and this,' said the messenger, putting into Elspat's
hand a small purse containing four or five dollars.

'He is gone, he is gone!' exclaimed Elspat. 'He has sold
himself to be the servant of the Saxons, and I shall never
more behold him! Tell me, Miles MacPhadraick, for now I
know you, is it the price of the son's blood that you have put
into the mother's hand?'

'Now, God forbid!' answered MacPhadraick, who was a
tacksman, and had possession of a considerable tract of
ground under his chief, a proprietor who lived about
twenty miles off—'God forbid I should do wrong, or say
wrong, to you, or to the son of MacTavish Mhor! I swear to
you by the hand of my chief that your son is well, and will
soon see you; and the rest he will tell you himself.' So
saying, MacPhadraick hastened back up the pathway, gained
the road, mounted his pony, and rode upon his way.

Chapter 3

Elspat MacTavish remained gazing on the money, as if the impress of the coin could have conveyed information how it was procured.

'I love not this MacPhadraick,' she said to herself; 'it was his race of whom the Bard hath spoken, saying, Fear them not when their words are loud as the winter's wind, but fear them when they fall on you like the sound of the thrush's song. And yet this riddle can be read but one way: My son hath taken the sword, to win that with strength like a man which churls would keep him from with the words that frighten children.' This idea, when once it occurred to her, seemed the more reasonable, that MacPhadraick, as she well knew, himself a cautious man, had so far encouraged her husband's practices as occasionally to buy cattle of MacTavish, although he must have well known how they were come by, taking care, however, that the transaction was so made as to be accompanied with great profit and absolute safety. Who so likely as MacPhadraick to indicate to a young cateran the glen in which he could commence his perilous trade with most prospect of success, who so likely to convert his booty into money? The feelings which another might have experienced on believing that an only son had rushed forward on the same path in which his father had perished were scarce known to the Highland mothers of that day. She thought of the death of MacTavish Mhor as that of a hero who had fallen in his proper trade of war, and who had not fallen unavenged. She feared less for her son's life than for his dishonour. She dreaded on his account the subjection to strangers, and the death-sleep of the soul which is brought on by what she regarded as slavery.

The moral principle which so naturally and so justly occurs to the mind of those who have been educated under a settled government of laws, that protect the property of the weak against the incursions of the strong, was to poor Elspat a book sealed and a fountain closed. She had been taught to consider those whom they called Saxons as a race with whom the Gael were constantly at war, and she regarded every settlement of theirs within the reach of Highland incursion as affording a legitimate object of attack and plunder. Her feelings on this point had been strengthened and confirmed, not only by the desire of revenge for the death of her husband, but by the sense of general indignation entertained, not unjustly, through the Highlands of Scotland, on account of the barbarous and violent conduct of the victors after the battle of Culloden. Other Highland clans, too, she regarded as the fair objects of plunder when that was possible, upon the score of ancient enmities and deadly feuds.

The prudence that might have weighed the slender means which the times afforded for resisting the efforts of a combined government, which had, in its less compact and established authority, been unable to put down the ravages of such lawless caterans as MacTavish Mhor, was unknown to a solitary woman, whose ideas still dwelt upon her own early times. She imagined that her son had only to proclaim himself his father's successor in adventure and enterprise, and that a force of men as gallant as those who had followed his father's banner would crowd around to support it when again displayed. To her, Hamish was the eagle who had only to soar aloft and resume his native place in the skies, without her being able to comprehend how many additional eyes would have watched his flight, how many additional bullets would have been directed at his bosom. To be brief, Elspat was one who viewed the present state of society with the same feelings with which she regarded the times that had passed away. She had been indigent, neglected, oppressed, since the days that her husband had no longer been feared and powerful, and she thought that the term of her ascendence would return when her son had determined to play the part of his father. If she permitted her eye to glance farther into futurity, it was but to anticipate that she must be for many a day cold in the grave, with the coronach of her tribe cried duly over her, before her fair-haired Hamish could, according to her calculation, die with his hand on the basket-hilt of the red claymore. His father's hair was grey, ere, after a hundred dangers, he had fallen with his arms in his hands—That she should have seen and survived the sight was a natural consequence of the manners of that age. And better it was—such was her proud thought—that she had seen him so die, than to have witnessed his departure from life in a smoky hovel—on a bed of rotten straw, like an overworn hound or a bullock which died of disease. But the hour of her young, her brave Hamish was yet far distant. He must succeed—he must conquer, like his father. And when he fell at length—for she anticipated for him no bloodless death—Elspat would ere then have lain long in the grave, and could neither see his death-struggle nor mourn over his grave-sod.

With such wild notions working in her brain, the spirit of Elspat rose to its usual pitch, or rather to one which seemed higher. In the emphatic language of Scripture, which in that idiom does not greatly differ from her own, she arose, she washed and changed her apparel, and ate bread, and was refreshed.

She longed eagerly for the return of her son, but she now longed with the bitter anxiety of doubt and apprehension. She said to herself, that much must be done ere he could in these times arise to be an eminent and dreaded leader. Yet when she saw him again, she almost expected him at the head of a daring band, with pipes playing and banners flying, the noble tartans fluttering free in the wind, in despite of the laws which had suppressed, under severe

penalties, the use of the national garb, and all the appurten-
ances of Highland chivalry. For all this, her eager imagination was content only to allow the interval of some days.

From the moment this opinion had taken deep and
serious possession of her mind, her thoughts were bent
upon receiving her son at the head of his adherents in the
manner in which she used to adorn her hut for the return of
his father.

The substantial means of subsistence she had not the
power of providing, nor did she consider that of importance. The successful caterans would bring with them herds
and flocks. But the interior of her hut was arranged for their
reception—the usquebaugh was brewed or distilled in a
larger quantity than it could have been supposed one
lone woman could have made ready. Her hut was put into
such order as might, in some degree, give it the appearance
of a day of rejoicing. It was swept and decorated with
boughs of various kinds, like the house of a Jewess upon
what is termed the Feast of the Tabernacles. The produce of
the milk of her little flock was prepared in as great variety of
forms as her skill admitted, to entertain her son and his
associates whom she expected to receive along with him.

But the principal decoration, which she sought with the
greatest toil, was the cloud-berry, a scarlet fruit, which is
only found on very high hills, and there only in small
quantities. Her husband, or perhaps one of his forefathers,
had chosen this as the emblem of his family, because it
seemed at once to imply by its scarcity the smallness of their
clan, and by the places in which it was found the ambitious
height of their pretentions.

For the time that these simple preparations of welcome
endured, Elspat was in a state of troubled happiness. In fact,
her only anxiety was that she might be able to complete all
that she could do to welcome Hamish and the friends who
she supposed must have attached themselves to his band

before they should arrive, and find her unprovided for their reception.

But when such efforts as she could make had been accomplished, she once more had nothing left to engage her save the trifling care of her goats; and when these had been attended to, she had only to review her little preparations, renew such as were of a transitory nature, replace decayed branches and fading boughs, and then to sit down at her cottage door and watch the road, as it ascended on the one side from the banks of the Awe, and on the other wound round the heights of the mountain, with such a degree of accommodation to hill and level as the plan of the military engineer permitted. While so occupied, her imagination, anticipating the future from recollections of the past, formed out of the morning mist or the evening cloud the wild forms of an advancing band, which were then called 'Sidier Dhu'—dark soldiers—dressed in their native tartan, and so named to distinguish them from the scarlet ranks of the British army. In this occupation she spent many hours of each morning and evening.

Chapter 4

It was in vain that Elspat's eyes surveyed the distant path, by the earliest light of the dawn and the latest glimmer of the twilight. No rising dust awakened the expectations of nodding plumes or flashing arms—the solitary traveller trudged listlessly along in his brown Lowland greatcoat, his tartans dyed black or purple, to comply with or evade the law which prohibited their being worn in their variegated hues. The spirit of the Gael, sunk and broken by the severe though perhaps necessary laws that proscribed the dress and arms which he considered as his birthright, was intimated by his drooping head and dejected appearance. Not in such depressed wanderers did Elspat recognise the light and free step of her son, now, as she concluded, regenerated from every sign of Saxon thraldom. Night by night, as darkness came, she removed from her unclosed door to throw herself on her restless pallet, not to sleep, but to watch. The brave and the terrible, she said, walk by night—their steps are heard in darkness, when all is silent save the whirlwind and the cataract—the timid deer comes only forth when the sun is upon the mountain's peak; but the bold wolf walks in the red light of the harvest-moon. She reasoned in vain—her son's expected summons did not call her from the lowly couch, where she lay dreaming of his approach. Hamish came not.

'Hope deferred,' saith the royal sage, 'maketh the heart sick;' and, strong as was Elspat's constitution, she began to experience that it was unequal to the toils to which her anxious and immoderate affection subjected her, when early one morning the appearance of a traveller on the lonely mountain-road revived hopes which had begun to sink into listless despair. There was no sign of Saxon subjugation about the stranger. At a distance she could see the flutter of the belted plaid, that drooped in graceful folds behind him, and the plume that, placed in the bonnet, showed rank and gentle birth. He carried a gun over his shoulder, the claymore was swinging by his side, with its usual appendages, the dirk, the pistol, and the *sporran mollach*. Ere yet her eye had scanned all these particulars, the light step of the traveller was hastened, his arm was waved in token of recognition—a moment more, and Elspat held in her arms her darling son, dressed in the garb of his ancestors, and looking, in her maternal eyes, the fairest among ten thousand.

The first outpouring of affection it would be impossible to describe. Blessings mingled with the most endearing epithets which her energetic language affords, in striving to express the wild rapture of Elspat's joy. Her board was heaped hastily with all she had to offer; and the mother watched the young soldier, as he partook of the refreshment, with feelings how similar to, yet how different from, those with which she had seen him draw his first sustenance from her bosom!

When the tumult of joy was appeased, Elspat became anxious to know her son's adventures since they parted, and could not help greatly censuring his rashness for traversing the hills in the Highland dress in the broad sunshine, when the penalty was so heavy, and so many red soldiers were abroad in the country.

'Fear not for me, mother,' said Hamish, in a tone designed to relieve her anxiety, and yet somewhat embarrassed; 'I may wear the *breacan* at the gate of Fort Augustus, if I like it.'

'Oh, be not too daring, my beloved Hamish, though it be the fault which best becomes thy father's son—yet be not too daring! Alas, they fight not now as in former days, with fair weapons and on equal terms, but take odds of numbers and of arms, so that the feeble and the strong are alike levelled by the shot of a boy. And do not think me unworthy to be called your father's widow, and your mother, because I speak thus; for God knoweth that, man to man, I would peril thee against the best in Breadalbane, and broad Lorn besides.'

'I assure you, my dearest mother,' replied Hamish, 'that I am in no danger. But have you seen MacPhadraick, mother, and what has he said to you on my account?'

'Silver he left with me in plenty, Hamish; but the best of his comfort was, that you were well, and would see me soon. But beware of MacPhadraick, my son; for when he called himself the friend of your father, he better loved the most worthless stirk in his herd than he did the life-blood of MacTavish Mhor. Use his services, therefore, and pay him for them—for it is thus we should deal with the unworthy; but take my counsel, and trust him not.'

Hamish could not suppress a sigh, which seemed to Elspat to intimate that the caution came too late. 'What have you done with him?' she continued, eager and alarmed. 'I had money of him, and he gives not that without value—he is none of those who exchange barley for chaff. Oh, if you repent you of your bargain, and if it be one which you may break off without disgrace to your truth or your manhood, take back his silver, and trust not to his fair words.'

'It may not be, mother,' said Hamish; 'I do not repent my engagement, unless that it must make me leave you soon.'

'Leave me! how leave me? Silly boy, think you I know not what duty belongs to the wife or mother of a daring man? Thou art but a boy yet; and when thy father had been the dread of the country for twenty years, he did not despise my company and assistance, but often said my help was worth that of two strong gillies.'

'It is not on that score, mother; but since I must leave the country'—

'Leave the country!' replied his mother, interrupting him. 'And think you that I am like a bush, that is rooted to the soil where it grows, and must die if carried elsewhere? I have breathed other winds than these of Ben Cruachan—I have followed your father to the wilds of Ross, and the impenetrable deserts of Y Mac Y Mhor—Tush, man, my limbs, old as they are, will bear me as far as your young feet can trace the way.'

'Alas, mother,' said the young man, with a faltering accent, 'but to cross the sea . . .'

'The sea! who am I that I should fear the sea? Have I never been in a birling in my life—never known the Sound of Mull, the Isles of Treshornish, and the rough rocks of Harris?'

'Alas, mother, I go far, far from all of these—I am enlisted in one of the new regiments, and we go against the French in America.'

'Enlisted!' uttered the astonished mother—'against *my* will—without *my* consent—You could not—you would not' —then rising up and assuming a posture of almost imperial command, 'Hamish, you DARED not!'

'Despair, mother, dares everything,' answered Hamish, in a tone of melancholy resolution. 'What should I do here, where I can scarce get bread for myself and you, and when the times are growing daily worse? Would you but sit down and listen, I would convince you I have acted for the best.'

With a bitter smile Elspat sat down, and the same severe ironical expression was on her features as, with her lips firmly closed, she listened to his vindication.

Hamish went on, without being disconcerted by her expected displeasure. 'When I left you, dearest mother, it was to go to MacPhadraick's house, for although I knew he is crafty and worldly, after the fashion of the Sassenach, yet he is wise, and I thought how he would teach me, as it would cost him nothing, in which way I could mend our estate in the world.'

'Our estate in the world!' said Elspat, losing patience at the word. 'And went you to a base fellow, with a soul no better than that of a cowherd, to ask counsel about your conduct? Your father asked none, save of his courage and his sword.'

'Dearest mother,' answered Hamish, 'how shall I convince you that you live in this land of our fathers as if our fathers were yet living? You walk as it were in a dream, surrounded by the phantoms of those who have been long with the dead. When my father lived and fought, the great respected the man of the strong right hand, and the rich feared him. He had protection from MacCallum More, and from Caberfae, and tribute from meaner men. That is ended, and his son would only earn a disgraceful and unpitied death, by the practices which gave his father credit and power among those who wear the breacan. The land is conquered—its lights are quenched—Glengarry, Lochiel, Perth, Lord Lewis, all the high chiefs are dead or in exile— We may mourn for it, but we cannot help it. Bonnet, broadsword, and sporran—power, strength, and wealth, were all lost on Drummossie Muir.'

'It is false!' said Elspat, fiercely. 'You, and such like dastardly spirits, are quelled by your own faint hearts, not by the strength of the enemy; you are like the fearful waterfowl, to whom the least cloud in the sky seems the shadow of the eagle.'

'Mother,' said Hamish, proudly, 'lay not faint heart on my charge. I go where men are wanted who have strong arms and bold hearts too. I leave a desert for a land where I may gather fame.'

'And you leave your mother to perish in want, age, and solitude,' said Elspat, essaying successively every means of moving a resolution which she began to see was more deeply rooted than she had at first thought.

'Not so, neither,' he answered; 'I leave you to comfort and certainty, which you have yet never known. Barcaldine's son is made a leader, and with him I have enrolled myself; MacPhadraick acts for him, and raises men, and finds his own in it.'

'That is the truest word of the tale, were all the rest as false as hell,' said the old woman bitterly.

'But we are to find our good in it also,' continued Hamish; 'for Barcaldine is to give you a shieling in his wood of Letterfindreight, with grass for your goats, and a cow, when you please to have one, on the common; and my own pay, dearest mother, though I am far away, will do more than provide you with meal, and with all else you can want.

Do not fear for me. I enter a private gentleman; but I will return, if hard fighting and regular duty can deserve it, an officer, and with half a dollar a day.'

'Poor child!' replied Elspat, in a tone of pity mingled with contempt. 'And you trust MacPhadraick?'

'I might, mother,' said Hamish, the dark red colour of his race crossing his forehead and cheeks, 'for MacPhadraick knows the blood which flows in my veins, and is aware that, should he break trust with you, he might count the days which could bring Hamish back to Breadalbane, and number those of his life within three suns more. I would kill him at his own hearth, did he break his word with me— I would, by the great Being who made us both!'

The look and attitude of the young soldier for a moment overawed Elspat; she was unused to see him express a deep and bitter mood, which reminded her so strongly of his father, but she resumed her remonstrances in the same taunting manner in which she had commenced them.

'Poor boy!' she said. 'And you think that at the distance of half the world your threats will be heard or thought of! But, go—go—place your neck under him of Hanover's yoke, against whom every true Gael fought to the death— Go, disown the royal Stuart, for whom your father, and his fathers, and your mother's fathers have crimsoned many a field with their blood.—Go, put your head under the belt of one of the race of Dermid, whose children murdered—Yes,' she added, with a wild shriek, 'murdered your mother's fathers in their peaceful dwellings in Glencoe!—Yes' she again exclaimed, with a wilder and shriller scream, 'I was then unborn, but my mother has told me—and I attended to the voice of *my* mother—well I remember her words!— They came in peace, and were received in friendship, and blood and fire arose, and screams and murder!'

'Mother,' answered Hamish, mournfully, but with a decided tone, 'all that I have thought ever—there is not a drop of the blood of Glencoe on the noble hand of Barcaldine—with the unhappy house of Glenlyon the curse remains, and on them God hath avenged it.'

'You speak like the Saxon priest already,' replied his mother. 'Will you not better stay, and ask a kirk from MacCallum More, that you may preach forgiveness to the race of Dermid?'

'Yesterday was yesterday,'answered Hamish, 'and to-day is to-day. When the clans are crushed and confounded together, it is well and wise that their hatreds and their feuds should not survive their independence and their power. He that cannot execute vengeance like a man should not harbour useless enmity like a craven. Mother, young Barcaldine is true and brave; I know that MacPhadraick counselled him that he should not let me take leave of you lest you dissuaded me from my purpose; but he said, 'Hamish MacTavish is the son of a brave man, and he will not break his word.' Mother, Barcaldine leads a hundred of the bravest of the sons of the Gael in their native dress, and with their fathers' arms—heart to heart—shoulder to shoulder. I have sworn to go with him—He has trusted me, and I will trust him.'

At this reply, so firmly and resolvedly pronounced, Elspat remained like one thunderstruck, and sunk in despair. The arguments which she had considered so irresistibly conclusive had recoiled like a wave from a rock. After a long pause, she filled her son's quaigh, and presented it to him with an air of dejected deference and submission.

'Drink,' she said, 'to thy father's roof-tree, ere you leave it for ever; and tell me—since the chains of a new king and of a new chief, whom your fathers knew not save as mortal enemies, are fastened upon the limbs of your father's son— tell me how many links you count upon them?'

Hamish took the cup, but looked at her as if uncertain of her meaning. She proceeded in a raised voice. 'Tell me,' she said, 'for I have a right to know, for how many days the will of those you have made your masters permits me to look upon you?—In other words, how many are the days of my life—for when you leave me the earth has naught besides worth living for!'

'Mother,' replied Hamish MacTavish, 'for six days I may remain with you, and, if you will set out with me on the fifth, I will conduct you in safety to your new dwelling. But if you remain here, then I will depart on the seventh by daybreak —then, as at the last moment, I MUST set out for Dumbarton, for if I appear not on the eighth day I am subject to punishment as a deserter, and am dishonoured as a soldier and a gentleman.'

'You father's foot,' she answered, 'was free as the wind on the heath—it were as vain to say to him where goest thou, as to ask that viewless driver of the clouds, Wherefore blowest thou? Tell me under what penalty thou must—since go thou must, and go thou wilt—return to thy thraldom?'

'Call it not thraldom, mother, it is the service of an honourable soldier—the only service which is now open to the son of MacTavish Mhor.'

'Yet say what is the penalty if thou shouldst not return?' replied Elspat.

'Military punishment as a deserter,' answered Hamish; writhing, however, as his mother failed not to observe, under some internal feelings, which she resolved to probe to the uttermost.

'And that,' she said, with assumed calmness, which her glancing eye disowned, 'is the punishment of a disobedient hound, is it not?'

'Ask me no more, mother,' said Hamish; 'the punishment is nothing to one who will never deserve it.'

'To me it is something,' replied Elspat, 'since I know better than thou that where there is power to inflict there is often the will to do so without cause. I would pray for thee,

Hamish, and I must know against what evils I should beseech Him who leaves none unguarded to protect thy youth and simplicity.'

'Mother,' said Hamish, 'it signifies little to what a criminal may be exposed, if a man is determined not to be such. Our Highland chiefs used also to punish their vassals, and, as I have heard, severely. Was it not Lachlan MacIan, whom we remember of old, whose head was struck off by order of his chieftain for shooting at the stag before him?'

'Ay,' said Elspat, 'and right he had to lose it, since he dishonoured the father of the people even in the face of the assembled clan. But the chiefs were noble in their ire—they punished with the sharp blade, and not with the baton. Their punishments drew blood, but they did not infer dishonour. Canst thou say the same for the laws under whose yoke thou hast placed thy freeborn neck?'

'I cannot—mother—I cannot,' said Hamish, mournfully 'I saw them punish a Sassenach for deserting, as they called it, his banner. He was scourged—I own it—scourged like a hound who has offended an imperious master. I was sick at the sight—I confess it. But the punishment of dogs is only for those worse than dogs, who know not how to keep their faith.'

'To this infamy, however, thou has subjected thyself, Hamish,' replied Elspat, 'if thou shouldst give, or thy officers take, measure of offence against thee.—I speak no more to thee on thy purpose.—Were the sixth day from this morning's sun my dying day, and thou wert to stay to close mine eyes, thou wouldst run the risk of being lashed like a dog at a post—yes! unless thou hadst the gallant heart to leave me to die alone, and upon my desolate hearth, the last spark of thy father's fire, and of thy forsaken mother's life, to be extinguished together!'—Hamish traversed the hut with an impatient and angry pace.

'Mother,' he said at length, 'concern not yourself about

such things. I cannot be subjected to such infamy, for never will I deserve it; and were I threatened with it, I should know how to die before I was so far dishonoured.'

'There spoke the son of the husband of my heart!' replied Elspat; and she changed the discourse, and seemed to listen in melancholy acquiescence, when her son reminded her how short the time was which they were permitted to pass in each other's society, and entreated that it might be spent without useless and unpleasant recollections respecting the circumstances under which they must soon be separated.

Elspat was now satisfied that her son, with some of his father's other properties, preserved the haughty masculine spirit which rendered it impossible to divert him from a resolution which he had deliberately adopted. She assumed, therefore, an exterior of apparent submission to their inevitable separation; and if she now and then broke out into complaints and murmurs, it was either that she could not altogether suppress the natural impetuosity of her temper, or because she had the wit to consider that a total and unreserved acquiscence might have seemed to her son constrained and suspicious, and induced him to watch and defeat the means by which she still hoped to prevent his leaving her. Her ardent though selfish affection for her son, incapable of being qualified by a regard for the true interests of the unfortunate object of her attachment, resembled the instinctive fondness of the animal race for their offspring; and, diving little further into futurity than one of the inferior creatures, she only felt that to be separated from Hamish was to die.

In the brief interval permitted them, Elspat exhausted every art which affection could devise to render agreeable to him the space which they were apparently to spend with each other. Her memory carried her far back into former days, and her stores of legendary history, which furnish at all times a principal amusement of the Highlander in his moments of repose, were augmented by an unusual acquaintance with the songs of ancient bards, and traditions of the most approved seannachies and tellers of tales. Her officious attentions to her son's accommodation, indeed, were so unremitted as almost to give him pain; and he endeavoured quietly to prevent her from taking so much personal toil in selecting the blooming heath for his bed, or preparing the meal for his refreshment. 'Let me alone, Hamish,' she would reply on such occasions; 'you follow your own will in departing from your mother, let your mother have hers in doing what gives her pleasure while you remain.'

So much she seemed to be reconciled to the arrangements which he had made in her behalf, that she could hear him speak to her of her removing to the lands of Green Colin, as the gentleman was called, on whose estate he had provided her an asylum. In truth, however, nothing could be further from her thoughts. From what he had said during their first violent dispute. Elspat had gathered that, if Hamish returned not by the appointed time permitted by his furlough, he would incur the hazard of corporal punishment. Were he placed within the risk of being thus dishonoured, she was well aware that he would never submit to the disgrace, by a return to the regiment where it might be inflicted. Whether she looked to any further probable consequences of her unhappy scheme cannot be known; but the partner of MacTavish Mhor in all his perils and wanderings was familiar with a hundred instances of resistance or escape, by which one brave man, amidst a land of rocks, lakes, and mountains, dangerous passes, and dark forests, might baffle the pursuit of hundreds. For the future, therefore, she feared nothing: her sole engrossing object was to prevent her son from keeping his word with his commanding officer.

With this secret purpose, she evaded the proposal which

Hamish repeatedly made, that they should set out together to take possession of her new abode; and she resisted it upon grounds apparently so natural to her character, that her son was neither alarmed nor displeased. 'Let me not,' she said, 'in the same short week, bid farewell to my only son, and to the glen in which I have so long dwelt. Let my eye, when dimmed with weeping for thee, still look around, for a while at least, upon Loch Awe and on Ben Cruachan.'

Hamish yielded the more willingly to his mother's humour in this particular, that one or two persons who resided in a neighbouring glen, and had given their sons to Barcaldine's levy, were also to be provided for on the estate of the chieftain, and it was apparently settled that Elspat was to take her journey along with them when they should remove to their new residence. Thus, Hamish believed that he had at once indulged his mother's humour and insured her safety and accommodation. But she nourished in her mind very different thoughts and projects!

The period of Hamish's leave of absence was fast approaching, and more than once he proposed to depart, in such time as to insure his gaining easily and early Dumbarton, the town where were the headquarters of his regiment. But still his mother's entreaties, his own natural disposition to linger among scenes long dear to him, and, above all, his firm reliance in his speed and activity, induced him to protract his departure till the sixth day, being the very last which he could possibly afford to spend with his mother, if indeed he meant to comply with the conditions of his furlough.

Chapter 5

But, for your son,—believe it, O, believe it—
Most dangerously you have with him prevailed,
If not most mortal to him.

Coriolanus.

On the evening which preceded his proposed departure Hamish walked down to the river with his fishing-rod, to practise in the Awe, for the last time, a sport in which he excelled, and to find, at the same time, the means for making one social meal with his mother on something better than their ordinary cheer. He was as successful as usual, and soon killed a fine salmon. On his return homeward an incident befell him which he afterwards related as ominous, though probably his heated imagination, joined to the universal turn of his countrymen for the marvellous, exaggerated into superstitious importance some very ordinary and accidental circumstance.

In the path which he pursued homeward he was surprised to observe a person who, like himself, was dressed and armed after the old Highland fashion. The first idea that struck him was that the passenger belonged to his own corps, who levied by government, and bearing arms under royal authority, were not amenable for breach of the statutes against the use of the Highland garb or weapons. But he was struck on perceiving, as he mended his pace to make up to his supposed comrade, meaning to request his company for the next day's journey, that the stranger wore a white cockade, the fatal badge which was proscribed in the High-lands. The stature of the man was tall, and there was something shadowy in the outline which added to his size; and his mode of motion, which rather resembled gliding than walking, impressed Hamish with superstitious fears concerning the character of the being which thus passed before him in the twilight. He no longer strove to make up to the stranger, but contented himself with keeping him in view, under the superstition common to the Highlanders, that you ought neither to intrude yourself on such supernatural apparitions as you may witness, nor avoid their presence, but leave it to themselves to withhold or extend their communication, as their power may permit, or the purpose of their commission require.

Upon an elevated knoll by the side of the road, just where the pathway turned down to Elspat's hut, the stranger made a pause, and seemed to await Hamish's coming up. Hamish, on his part, seeing it was necessary he should pass the object of his suspicion, mustered up his courage, and approached the spot where the stranger had placed himself; who first pointed to Elspat's hut, and made, with arm and head, a gesture prohibiting Hamish to approach it, then stretched his hand to the road which led to the southward, with a motion which seemed to enjoin his instant departure in that direction. In a moment afterwards the plaided form was gone—Hamish did not exactly say vanished, because there were rocks and stunted trees enough to have concealed him; but it was his own opinion that he had seen the spirit of MacTavish Mhor, warning him to commence his instant journey to Dumbarton, without waiting till morning, or again visiting his mother's hut.

In fact, so many accidents might arise to delay his journey, especially where there were many ferries, that it became his settled purpose, though he could not depart without bidding his mother adieu, that he neither could nor would abide longer than for that object; and that the first glimpse of next day's sun should see him many miles advanced towards Dumbarton. He descended the path, therefore, and entering the cottage, he communicated in a hasty and troubled voice, which indicated mental agitation, his determination to take his instant departure. Somewhat to his surprise, Elspat appeared not to combat his purpose, but she urged him to take some refreshment ere he left her for ever. He did so hastily, and in silence, thinking on the approaching separation, and scarce yet believing it would take place without a final struggle with his mother's fondness. To his surprise, she filled the quaigh with liquor for his parting cup.

'Go,' she said, 'my son, since such is thy settled purpose; but first stand once more on thy mother's hearth, the flame on which will be extinguished long ere thy foot shall again be placed there.'

'To your health, mother!' said Hamish, 'and may we meet again in happiness, in spite of your ominous words.'

'It were better not to part,' said his mother, watching him as he quaffed the liquor, of which he would have held it ominous to have left a drop.

'And now,' she said, muttering the words to herself, 'go—if you canst go.'

'Mother,' said Hamish, as he replaced on the table the empty quaigh, 'thy drink is pleasant to the taste, but it takes away the strength which it ought to give.'

'Such is its first effect, my son,' replied Elspat; 'but lie down upon that soft heather couch, shut your eyes but for a moment, and, in the sleep of an hour, you shall have more refreshment than in the ordinary repose of three whole nights, could they be blended into one.'

'Mother,' said Hamish, upon whose brain the potion was now taking effect, 'give me my bonnet—I must kiss you and begone—yet it seems as if my feet were nailed to the floor.'

'Indeed,' said his mother, 'you will be instantly well, if you will sit down for half an hour—but half an hour; it is eight hours to dawn, and dawn were time enough for your father's son to begin such a journey.'

'I must obey you, mother—I feel I must,' said Hamish,

inarticulately; 'but call me when the moon rises.'

He sat down on the bed—reclined back, and almost instantly was fast asleep. With the throbbing glee of one who has brought to an end a difficult and troublesome enterprise, Elspat proceeded tenderly to arrange the plaid of the unconscious slumberer, to whom her extravagant affection was doomed to be so fatal, expressing, while busied in her office, her delight, in tones of mingled tenderness and triumph. 'Yes,' she said, 'calf of my heart, the moon shall arise and set to thee, and so shall the sun; but not to light thee from the land of thy fathers, or tempt thee to serve the foreign prince or the feudal enemy! To no son of Dermid shall I be delivered, to be fed like a bondswoman; but he who is my pleasure and my pride shall be my guard and my protector. They say the Highlands are changed; but I see Ben Cruachan rear his crest as high as ever into the evening sky—no one hath yet herded his kine on the depth of Loch Awe—and yonder oak does not yet bend like a willow. The children of the mountains will be such as their fathers, until the mountains themselves be levelled with the strath. In these wild forests, which used to support thousands of the brave, there is still surely subsistence and refuge left for one aged woman and one gallant youth, of the ancient race and the ancient manners.'

While the misjudging mother thus exulted in the success of her stratagem, we may mention to the reader that it was founded on the acquaintance with drugs and simples, which Elspat, accomplished in all things belonging to the wild life which she had led, possessed in an uncommon degree, and which she exercised for various purposes. With the herbs, which she knew how to select as well as how to distil, she could relieve more diseases than a regular medical person could easily believe. She applied some to dye the bright colours of the tartan—from others she compounded draughts of various powers, and unhappily possessed the secret of one which was strongly soporific. Upon the effects of this last concoction, as the reader doubtless has anticipated, she reckoned with security on delaying Hamish beyond the period for which his return was appointed; and she trusted to his horror for the apprehended punishment to which he was thus rendered liable, to prevent him from returning at all.

Sound and deep, beyond natural rest, was the sleep of Hamish MacTavish on that eventful evening, but not such the repose of his mother. Scarce did she close her eyes from time to time, but she awakened again with a start, in the terror that her son had arisen and departed; and it was only on approaching his couch, and hearing his deep-drawn and regular breathing, that she reassured herself of the security of the repose in which he was plunged.

Still, dawning, she feared, might awaken him, notwithstanding the unusual strength of the potion with which she had drugged his cup. If there remained a hope of mortal man accomplishing the journey, she was aware that Hamish would attempt it, though he were to die from fatigue upon the road. Animated by this new fear, she studied to exclude the light, by stopping all the crannies and crevices through which, rather than through any regular entrance, the morning beams might find access to her miserable dwelling; and this in order to detain amid its wants and wretchedness the being on whom, if the world itself had been at her disposal, she would have joyfully conferred it.

Her pains were bestowed unnecessarily. The sun rose high above the heavens, and not the fleetest stag in Breadalbane, were the hounds at his heels, could have sped, to save his life, so fast as would have been necessary to keep Hamish's appointment. Her purpose was fully attained—her son's return within the period assigned was impossible. She deemed it equally impossible that he would ever dream of returning, standing, as he must now do, in the danger of an infamous punishment. By degrees, and at different times, she had gained from him a full acquaintance with the predicament in which he would be placed by failing to appear on the day appointed, and the very small hope he could entertain of being treated with lenity.

It is well known that the great and wise Earl of Chatham prided himself on the scheme by which he drew together for the defence of the colonies those hardy Highlanders who, until his time, had been the objects of doubt, fear, and suspicion, on the part of each successive administration. But some obstacles occurred, from the peculiar habits and temper of this people, to the execution of his patriotic project. By nature and habit, every Highlander was accustomed to the use of arms, but at the same time totally unaccustomed to, and impatient of, the restraints imposed by discipline upon regular troops. They were a species of militia, who had no conception of a camp as their only home. If a battle was lost, they dispersed to save themselves, and look out for the safety of their families; if won, they went back to their glens to hoard up their booty, and attend to their cattle and their farms. This privilege of going and coming at pleasure they would not be deprived of even by their chiefs, whose authority was in most other respects so despotic. It followed, as a matter of course, that the new-levied Highland recruits could scarce be made to comprehend the nature of a military engagement, which compelled a man to serve in the army longer than he pleased; and perhaps, in many instances, sufficient care was not taken at enlisting to explain to them the permanency of the engagement which they came under, lest such a disclosure should induce them to change their mind. Desertions were therefore become numerous from the newly raised regiment, and the veteran general who commanded at Dumbarton saw no better way of checking them than by causing an unusually severe example to be made of a deserter from an English corps. The young Highland regiment was obliged to attend upon the punishment, which struck a people, peculiarly jealous of personal honour, with equal horror and disgust, and not unnaturally indisposed some of them to the service. The old general, however, who had been regularly bred in the German wars, stuck to his own opinion, and gave out in orders that the first Highlander who might either desert, or fail to appear at the expiry of his furlough, should be brought to the halberds, and punished like the culprit whom they had seen in that condition. No man doubted that General —— would keep his word rigorously whenever severity was required, and Elspat, therefore, knew that her son, when he perceived that due compliance with his orders was impossible, must at the same time consider the degrading punishment denounced against his defection as inevitable, should he place himself within the general's power.

When noon was well passed, new apprehensions came on the mind of the lonely woman. Her son still slept under the influence of the draught; but what if, being stronger than she had ever known it administered, his health or his reason should be affected by its potency? For the first time, likewise, notwithstanding her high ideas on the subject of parental authority, she began to dread the resentment of her son, whom her heart told her she had wronged. Of late, she had observed that his temper was less docile, and his determinations, especially upon this late occasion of his enlistment, independently formed, and then boldly carried through. She remembered the stern wilfulness of his father when he accounted himself ill-used, and began to dread that Hamish, upon finding the deceit she had put upon him, might resent it even to the extent of casting her off, and pursuing his own course through the world alone. Such were the alarming and yet the reasonable apprehensions which began to crowd upon the unfortunate woman, after the apparent success of her ill-advised stratagem.

It was near evening when Hamish first awoke, and then he was far from being in full possession either of his mental or bodily powers. From his vague expressions and disordered pulse, Elspat at first experienced much apprehension; but she used such expedients as her medical knowledge suggested; and in the course of the night she had the satisfaction to see him sink once more into a deep sleep, which probably carried off the greater part of the effects of the drug, for about sun-rising she heard him arise and call to her for his bonnet. This she had purposely removed, from a fear that he might awaken and depart in the night-time, without her knowledge.

'My bonnet—my bonnet,'cried Hamish, 'it is time to take farewell. Mother, your drink was too strong—the sun is up —but with the next morning I will still see the double summit of the ancient Dun. My bonnet—my bonnet! mother, I must be instant in my departure.' These expressions made it plain that poor Hamish was unconscious that two nights and a day had passed since he had drained the fatal quaigh, and Elspat had now to venture on what she felt as the almost perilous as well as painful task of explaining her machinations.

'Forgive me, my son,' she said, approaching Hamish, and taking him by the hand with an air of deferential awe, which perhaps she had not always used to his father, even when in his moody fits.

'Forgive you, mother—for what?' said Hamish, laughing; 'for giving me a dram that was too strong, and which my head still feels this morning, or for hiding my bonnet to keep me an instant longer? Nay, do *you* forgive *me*. Give me the bonnet, and let that be done which now must be done. Give me my bonnet, or I go without it; surely I am not to be delayed by so trifling a want as that—I, who have gone for years with only a strap of deer's hide to tie back my hair.

Trifle not, but give it me, or I must go bareheaded, since to stay is impossible.'

'My son,' said Elspat, keeping fast hold of his hand, 'what is done cannot be recalled; could you borrow the wings of yonder eagle, you would arrive at the Dun too late for what you purpose—too soon for what awaits you there. You believe you see the sun rising for the first time since you have seen him set, but yesterday beheld him climb Ben Cruachan, though your eyes were closed to his light.'

Hamish cast upon his mother a wild glance of extreme terror, then, instantly recovering himself, said—'I am no child to be cheated out of my purpose by such tricks as these —Farewell, mother, each moment is worth a lifetime.'

'Stay,' she said, 'my dear—my deceived son! Rush not on infamy and ruin—Yonder I see the priest upon the high-road on his white horse—ask him the day of the month and the week—let him decide between us.'

With the speed of an eagle Hamish darted up the acclivity, and stood by the minister of Glenorchy, who was pacing out thus early to administer consolation to a distressed family near Bunawe.

The good man was somewhat startled to behold an armed Highlander, then so unusual a sight, and apparently much agitated, stop his horse by the bridle, and ask him with a faltering voice the day of the week and the month. 'Had you been where you should have been yesterday, young man,' replied the clergyman, 'you would have known that it was God's Sabbath; and that this is Monday, the second day of the week, and twenty-first of the month.'

'And this is true?' said Hamish.

'As true,' answered the surprised minister, 'as that I yesterday preached the word of God to this parish.—What ails you, young man? Are you sick? Are you in your right mind?'

Hamish made no answer, only repeated to himself the

first expression of the clergyman—'Had you been where you should have been yesterday;' and, so saying, he let go the bridle, turned from the road, and descended the path towards the hut, with the look and pace of one who was going to execution. The minister looked after him with surprise; but although he knew the inhabitant of the hovel, the character of Elspat had not invited him to open any communication with her, because she was generally reputed a Papist, or rather one indifferent to all religion, except some superstitious observances which had been handed down from her parents. On Hamish the Reverend Mr. Tyrie had bestowed instructions when he was occasionally thrown in his way, and, if the seed fell among the brambles and thorns of a wild and uncultivated disposition, it had not yet been entirely checked or destroyed. There was something so ghastly in the present expression of the youth's features, that the good man was tempted to go down to the hovel and inquire whether any distress had befallen the inhabitants, in which his presence might be consoling and his ministry useful. Unhappily he did not persevere in this resolution, which might have saved a great misfortune, as he would have probably become a mediator for the unfortunate young man; but a recollection of the wild moods of such Highlanders as had been educated after the old fashion of the country prevented his interesting himself in the widow and son of the far-dreaded robber MacTavish Mhor; and he thus missed an opportunity, which he afterwards sorely repented, of doing much good.

When Hamish MacTavish entered his mother's hut, it was only to throw himself on the bed he had left, and, exclaiming, 'Undone, undone!' to give vent, in cries of grief and anger, to his deep sense of the deceit which had been practised on him, and of the cruel predicament to which he was reduced.

Elspat was prepared for the first explosion of her son's

passion, and said to herself, 'It is but the mountain torrent, swelled by the thunder shower. Let us sit and rest us by the bank; for all its present tumult, the time will soon come when we may pass it dryshod.' She suffered his complaints and his reproaches, which were, even in the midst of his agony, respectful and affectionate, to die away without returning any answer; and when, at length, having exhausted all the exclamations of sorrow which his language, copious in expressing the feelings of the heart, affords to the sufferer, he sank into a gloomy silence, she suffered the interval to continue near an hour ere she approached her son's coach.

'And now,' she said at length, with a voice in which the authority of the mother was qualified by her tenderness, 'Have you exhausted your idle sorrows, and are you able to place what you have gained against what you have lost? Is the false son of Dermid your brother, or the father of your tribe, that you weep because you cannot bind yourself to his belt, and become one of those who must do his bidding? Could you find in yonder distant country the lakes and the mountains that you leave behind you here? Can you hunt the deer of Breadalbane in the forests of America, or will the ocean afford you the silver-scaled salmon of the Awe? Consider, then, what is your loss, and, like a wise man, set it against what you have won.'

'I have lost all, mother,' replied Hamish, 'since I have broken my word, and lost my honour. I might tell my tale, but who—oh, who would believe me?' The unfortunate young man again clasped his hands together, and, pressing them to his forehead, hid his face upon the bed.

Elspat was now really alarmed, and perhaps wished the fatal deceit had been left unattempted. She had no hope or refuge saving in the eloquence of persuasion, of which she possessed no small share, though her total ignorance of the world as it actually existed rendered its energy unavailing.

She urged her son, by every tender epithet which a parent could bestow, to take care for his own safety.

'Leave me,' she said, 'to baffle your pursuers. I will save your life—I will save your honour—I will tell them that my fair-haired Hamish fell from the Corrie dhu (black precipice) into the gulf, of which human eye never beheld the bottom. I will tell them this, and I will fling your plaid on the thorns which grow on the brink of the precipice, that they may believe my words. They will believe, and they will return to the Dun of the double-crest; for though the Saxon drum can call the living to die, it cannot recall the dead to their slavish standard. Then we will travel together far northward to the salt lakes of Kintail, and place glens and mountains betwixt us and the sons of Dermid. We will visit the shores of the dark lake, and my kinsmen—(for was not my mother of the children of Kenneth, and will they not remember us with the old love?)—my kinsmen will receive us with the affection of the olden time, which lives in those distant glens, where the Gael still dwell in their nobleness, unmingled with the churl Saxons, or with the base brood that are their tools and their slaves.'

The energy of the language, somewhat allied to hyperbole, even in its most ordinary expressions, now seemed almost too weak to afford Elspat the means of bringing out the splendid picture which she presented to her son of the land in which she proposed to him to take refuge. Yet the colours were few with which she could paint her Highland paradise. 'The hills,' she said, 'were higher and more magnificent than those of Breadalbane—Ben Cruachan was but a dwarf to Skooroora. The lakes were broader and larger, and abounded not only with fish, but with the enchanted and amphibious animal which gives oil to the lamp. The deer were larger and more numerous—the white-tusked boar, the chase of which the brave loved best, was yet to be roused in those western solitudes—the men were nobler,

wiser, and stronger than the degenerate brood who lived
under the Saxon banner. The daughters of the land were
beautiful, with blue eyes and hair, and bosoms of snow, and
out of these she would choose a wife for Hamish, of blame-
less descent, spotless fame, fixed and true affection, who
should be in their summer bothy as a beam of the sun, and
in their winter abode as the warmth of the needful fire.'

Such were the topics with which Elspat strove to soothe
the despair of her son, and to determine him, if possible, to
leave the fatal spot, on which he seemed resolved to linger.
The style of her rhetoric was poetical, but in other respects
resembled that which, like other fond mothers, she had
lavished on Hamish, while a child or a boy, in order to gain
his consent to do something he had no mind to; and she
spoke louder, quicker, and more earnestly, in proportion as
she began to despair of her words carrying conviction.

On the mind of Hamish her eloquence made no
impression. He knew far better than she did the actual
situation of the country, and was sensible, that, though it
might be possible to hide himself as a fugitive among more
distant mountains, there was now no corner in the Highlands in which his father's profession could be practised,
even if he had not adopted, from the improved ideas of the
time when he lived, the opinion that the trade of the cateran
was no longer the road to honour and distinction. Her
words were therefore poured into regardless ears, and she
exhausted herself in vain in the attempt to paint the region
of her mother's kinsmen in such terms as might tempt
Hamish to accompany her thither. She spoke for hours, but
she spoke in vain. She could extort no answer, save groans,
and sighs, and ejaculations, expressing the extremity of
despair.

At length, starting on her feet, and changing the
monotonous tone in which she had chanted, as it were, the
praises of the province of refuge, into the short, stern

language of eager passion—'I am a fool,' she said, 'to spend my words upon an idle, poor-spirited, unintelligent boy, who crouches like a hound to the lash. Wait here, and receive your taskmasters, and abide your chastisement at their hands; but do not think your mother's eyes will behold it. I could not see it and live. My eyes have looked often upon death, but never upon dishonour. Farewell, Hamish!—We never meet again.'

She dashed from the hut like a lapwing, and perhaps for the moment actually entertained the purpose which she expressed, of parting with her son for ever. A fearful sight she would have been that evening to any who might have met her wandering through the wilderness like a restless spirit, and speaking to herself in language which will endure no translation. She rambled for hours, seeking rather than shunning the most dangerous paths. The precarious track through the morass, the dizzy path along the edge of the precipice, or by the banks of the gulfing river, were the roads which, far from avoiding, she sought with eagerness, and traversed with reckless haste. But the courage arising from despair was the means of saving the life which (though deliberate suicide was rarely practised in the Highlands) she was perhaps desirous of terminating. Her step on the verge of the precipice was firm as that of the wild goat. Her eye, in that state of excitation, was so keen as to discern, even amid darkness, the perils which noon would not have enabled a stranger to avoid.

Elspat's course was not directly forward, else she had soon been far from the bothy in which she had left her son. It was circuitous, for that hut was the centre to which her heart-strings were chained, and, though she wandered around it, she felt it impossible to leave the vicinity. With the first beams of morning she returned to the hut. A while she paused at the wattled door, as if ashamed that lingering fondness should have brought her back to the spot which she had left with the purpose of never returning; but there was yet more of fear and anxiety in her hesitation—of anxiety lest her fair-haired son had suffered from the effects of her potion—of fear lest his enemies had come upon him in the night. She opened the door of the hut gently, and entered with noiseless step. Exhausted with his sorrow and anxiety, and not entirely relieved perhaps from the influence of the powerful opiate, Hamish Bean again slept the stern sound sleep by which the Indians are said to be overcome during the interval of their torments. His mother was scarcely sure that she actually discerned his form on the bed, scarce certain that her ear caught the sound of his breathing. With a throbbing heart Elspat went to the fireplace in the centre of the hut, where slumbered, covered with a piece of turf, the glimmering embers of the fire, never extinguished on a Scottish hearth until the indwellers leave the mansion for ever.

'Feeble greishogh,' she said, as she lighted, by the help of a match, a splinter of bog pine which was to serve the place of a candle; 'weak greishogh, soon shalt thou be put out for ever, and may Heaven grant that the life of Elspat MacTavish have no longer duration than thine!'

While she spoke she raised the blazing light towards the bed, on which still lay the prostrate limbs of her son, in a posture that left it doubtful whether he slept or swooned. As she advanced towards him the light flashed upon his eyes— he started up in an instant, made a stride forward with his naked dirk in his hand, like a man armed to meet a mortal enemy, and exclaimed, 'Stand off!—on thy life, stand off!'

'It is the word and the action of my husband,' answered Elspat; 'and I know by his speech and his step the son of MacTavish Mhor.'

'Mother,' said Hamish, relapsing from his tone of desperate firmness into one of melancholy expostulation— 'oh, dearest mother, wherefore have you returned hither?'

'Ask why the hind comes back to the fawn,' said Elspat; 'why the cat of the mountain returns to her lodge and her young. Know you, Hamish, that the heart of the mother only lives in the bosom of the child.'

'Then will it soon cease to throb,' said Hamish, 'unless it can beat within a bosom that lies beneath the turf.—Mother, do not blame me; if I weep, it is not for myself but for you, for my sufferings will soon be over; but yours—Oh, who but Heaven shall set a boundary to them!'

Elspat shuddered and stepped backward, but almost instantly resumed her firm and upright position and her dauntless bearing.

'I thought thou wert a man but even now,' she said, 'and thou art again a child. Hearken to me yet, and let us leave this place together. Have I done thee wrong or injury? If so, yet do not avenge it so cruelly—See, Elspat MacTavish, who never kneeled before even a priest, falls prostrate before her own son, and craves his forgiveness.' And at once she threw herself on her knees before the young man, seized on his hand, and, kissing it a hundred times, repeated as often, in heartbreaking accents, the most earnest entreaties for forgiveness. 'Pardon,' she exclaimed, 'pardon, for the sake of your father's ashes—pardon, for the sake of the pain with which I bore thee, the care with which I nurtured thee!—Hear it, Heaven, and behold it, Earth—the mother asks pardon of her child, and she is refused!'

It was in vain that Hamish endeavoured to stem this tide of passion, by assuring his mother, with the most solemn asseverations, that he forgave entirely the fatal deceit which she had practised upon him.

'Empty words,' she said; 'idle protestations, which are but used to hide the obduracy of your resentment. Would you have me believe you, then leave the hut this instant, and retire from a country which every hour renders more dangerous.—Do this, and I may think you have forgiven me

—refuse it, and again I call on moon and stars, heaven and earth, to witness the unrelenting resentment with which you prosecute your mother for a fault which, if it be one, arose out of love to you.'

'Mother,' said Hamish, 'on this subject you move me not. I will fly before no man. If Barcaldine should send every Gael that is under his banner, here, and in this place, will I abide them; and when you bid me fly, you may as well command yonder mountain to be loosened from its foundations. Had I been sure of the road by which they are coming hither, I had spared them the pains of seeking me; but I might go by the mountain, while they perchance came by the lake. Here I will abide my fate; nor is there in Scotland a voice of power enough to bid me stir from hence, and be obeyed.'

'Here, then, I also stay,' said Elspat, rising up and speaking with assumed composure. 'I have seen my husband's death—my eyelids shall not grieve to look on the fall of my son. But MacTavish Mhor died as became the brave, with his good sword in his right hand; my son will perish like the bullock that is driven to the shambles by the Saxon owner who has bought him for a price.'

'Mother,' said the unhappy young man, 'you have taken my life; to that you have a right, for you gave it; but touch not my honour! It came to me from a brave train of ancestors, and should be sullied neither by man's deed nor woman's speech. What I shall do, perhaps I myself yet know not; but tempt me no further by reproachful words; you have already made wounds more than you can ever heal.'

'It is well, my son,' said Elspat, in reply. 'Expect neither further complaint nor remonstrance from me; but let us be silent, and wait the chance which Heaven shall send us.'

The sun arose on the next morning, and found the bothy silent as the grave. The mother and son had arisen, and were engaged each in their separate task—Hamish in preparing and cleaning his arms with the greatest accuracy, but with an air of deep dejection. Elspat more restless in her agony of spirit, employed herself in making ready the food which the distress of yesterday had induced them both to dispense with for an unusual number of hours. She placed it on the board before her son so soon as it was prepared, with the words of a Gaelic poet, 'Without daily food, the husbandman's ploughshare stands still in the furrow; without daily food, the sword of the warrior is too heavy for his hand. Our bodies are our slaves, yet they must be fed if we would have their service. So spake in ancient days the Blind Bard to the warriors of Fion.'

The young man made no reply, but he fed on what was placed before him, as if to gather strength for the scene which he was to undergo. When his mother saw that he had eaten what sufficed him, she again filled the fatal quaigh, and proffered it as the conclusion of the repast. But he started aside with a convulsive gesture, expressive at once of fear and abhorrence.

'Nay, my son,' she said, 'this time, surely, thou hast no cause of fear.'

'Urge me not, mother,' answered Hamish; 'or put the leprous toad into a flagon, and I will drink; but from that accursed cup, and of that mind-destroying potion, never will I taste more!'

'At your pleasure, my son,' said Elspat, haughtily, and began, with much apparent assiduity, the various domestic tasks which had been interrupted during the preceding day. Whatever was at her heart, all anxiety seemed banished from her looks and demeanour. It was but from an over-activity of bustling exertion that it might have been perceived, by a close observer, that her actions were spurred by some internal cause of painful excitement; and such a spectator, too, might also have observed how often she broke off the snatches of songs or tunes which she hummed, apparently without knowing what she was doing, in order to cast a hasty glance from the door of the hut. Whatever might be in the mind of Hamish, his demeanour was directly the reverse of that adopted by his mother. Having finished the task of cleaning and preparing his arms, which he arranged within the hut, he sat himself down before the door of the bothy, and watched the opposite hill, like the fixed sentinel who expects the approach of an enemy. Noon found him in the same unchanged posture, and it was an hour after that period, when his mother, standing beside him, laid her hand on his shoulder, and said, in a tone indifferent, as if she had been talking of some friendly visit, 'When dost thou expect them?'

'They cannot be here till the shadows fall long to the eastward,' replied Hamish; 'that is, even supposing the nearest party, commanded by Sergeant Allan Breack Cameron, has been commanded hither by express from Dumbarton, as it is most likely they will.'

'Then enter beneath your mother's roof once more; partake the last time of the food which she has prepared; after this, let them come, and thou shalt see if thy mother is a useless incumbrance in the day of strife. Thy hand, practised as it is, cannot fire these arms so fast as I can load them; nay, if it is necessary, I do not myself fear the flash or report, and my aim has been held fatal.'

'In the name of Heaven, mother, meddle not with this matter!' said Hamish. 'Allan Breack is a wise man and a kind one, and comes of a good stem. It may be, he can promise for our officers, that they will touch me with no infamous punishment; and if they offer me confinement in the dungeon, or death by the musket, to that I may not object.'

'Alas, and wilt thou trust to their word, my foolish child? Remember the race of Dermid were ever fair and false, and no sooner shall they have gyves on thy hands than they will strip thy shoulders for the scourge.'

'Save your advice, mother,' said Hamish, sternly; 'for me, my mind is made up.'

But though he spoke thus, to escape the almost persecuting urgency of his mother, Hamish would have found it, at that moment, impossible to say upon what course of conduct he had thus fixed. On one point alone he was determined—namely, to abide his destiny, be what it might, and not to add to the breach of his word, of which he had been involuntarily rendered guilty, by attempting to escape from punishment. This act of self-devotion he conceived to be due to his own honour, and that of his countrymen. Which of his comrades would in future be trusted, if he should be considered as having broken his word, and betrayed the confidence of his officers? and whom but Hamish Bean MacTavish would the Gael accuse, for having verified and confirmed the suspicions which the Saxon general was well known to entertain against the good faith of the Highlanders? He was, therefore, bent firmly to abide his fate. But whether his intention was to yield himself peaceably into the hands of the party who should come to apprehend him, or whether he purposed, by a show of resistance, to provoke them to kill him on the spot, was a question which he could not himself have answered. His desire to see Barcaldine, and explain the cause of his absence at the appointed time, urged him to the one course; his fear of the degrading punishment, and of his mother's bitter upbraidings, strongly instigated the latter and the more dangerous purpose. He left it to chance to decide when the crisis should arrive; nor did he tarry long in expectation of the catastrophe.

Evening approached, the gigantic shadows of the mountains streamed in darkness towards the east, while their western peaks were still glowing with crimson and gold. The road which winds round Ben Cruachan was fully visible from the door of the bothy, when a party of five

Highland soldiers, whose arms glanced in the sun, wheeled suddenly into sight from the most distant extremity, where the highway is hidden behind the mountain. One of the party walked a little before the other four, who marched regularly and in files, according to the rules of military discipline. There was no dispute, from the firelocks which they carried, and the plaids and bonnets which they wore, that they were a party of Hamish's regiment, under a non-commissioned officer; and there could be as little doubt of the purpose of their appearance on the banks of Loch Awe.

'They come briskly forward,' said the widow of MacTavish Mhor. 'I wonder how fast or how slow some of them will return again! But they are five, and it is too much odds for a fair field. Step back within the hut, my son, and shoot from the loophole beside the door. Two you may bring down ere they quit the high-road for the footpath—there will remain but three; and your father, with my aid, has often stood against that number.'

Hamish Bean took the gun which his mother offered, but did not stir from the door of the hut. He was soon visible to the party on the high-road, as was evident from their increasing their pace to a run; the files, however, still keeping together like coupled greyhounds, and advancing with great rapidity. In far less time than would have been accomplished by men less accustomed to the mountains, they had left the high-road, traversed the narrow path, and approached within pistol-shot of the bothy, at the door of which stood Hamish, fixed like a statue of stone, with his firelock in his hand, while his mother, placed behind him, and almost driven to frenzy by the violence of her passions, reproached him, in the strongest terms which despair could invent, for his want of resolution and faintness of heart. Her words increased the bitter gall which was arising in the young man's own spirit, as he observed the unfriendly speed with which his late comrades were eagerly making towards him, like hounds towards the stag when he is at bay. The untamed and angry passions which he inherited from father and mother were awakened by the supposed hostility of those who pursued him; and the restraint under which these passions had been hitherto held by his sober judgement began gradually to give way. The sergeant now called to him, 'Hamish Bean MacTavish, lay down your arms and surrender.'

'Do *you* stand, Allan Breack Cameron, and command your men to stand, or it will be the worse for us all.'

'Halt, men!' said the sergeant, but continuing himself to advance. 'Hamish, think what you do, and give up your gun; you may spill blood, but you cannot escape punishment.'

'The scourge—the scourge—my son, beware the scourge!' whispered his mother.

'Take heed, Allan Breack,' said Hamish, 'I would not hurt you willingly, but I will not be taken unless you can assure me against the Saxon lash.'

'Fool!' answered Cameron, 'you know I cannot. Yet I will do all I can. I will say I met you on your return, and the punishment will be light—but give up you musket—Come on, men.'

Instantly he rushed forward, extending his arm as if to push aside the young man's levelled firelock. Elspat exclaimed, 'Now, spare not your father's blood to defend your father's hearth!' Hamish fired his piece, and Cameron dropped dead.—All these things happened, it might be said, in the same moment of time. The soldiers rushed forward and seized Hamish, who, seeming petrified with what he had done, offered not the least resistance. Not so his mother, who, seeing the men about to put handcuffs on her son, threw herself on the soldiers with such fury that it required two of them to hold her, while the rest secured the prisoner.

'Are you not an accursed creature,' said one of the men to

Hamish, 'to have slain your best friend, who was contriving, during the whole march, how he could find some way of getting you off without punishment for your desertion?'

'Do you hear *that,* mother?' said Hamish, turning himself as much towards her as his bonds would permit—but the mother heard nothing, and saw nothing. She had fainted on the floor of her hut. Without waiting for her recovery, the party almost immediately began their homeward march towards Dumbarton, leading along with them their prisoner. They thought it necessary, however, to stay for a little space at the village of Dalmally, from which they despatched a party of the inhabitants to bring away the body of their unfortunate leader, while they themselves repaired to a magistrate to state what had happened, and require his instructions as to the further course to be pursued. The crime being of a military character, they were instructed to march the prisoner to Dumbarton without delay.

The swoon of the mother of Hamish lasted for a length of time; the longer perhaps that her constitution, strong as it was, must have been much exhausted by her previous agitation of three days' endurance. She was roused from her stupor at length by female voices, which cried the coronach, or lament for the dead, with clapping of hands and loud exclamations; while the melancholy note of a lament, appropriate to the clan Cameron, played on the bagpipe, was heard from time to time.

Elspat started up like one awakened from the dead, and without any accurate recollection of the scene which had passed before her eyes. There were females in the hut who were swathing the corpse in its bloody plaid before carrying it from the fatal spot. 'Women,' she said, starting up and interrupting their chant at once and their labour—'Tell me, women, why sing you the dirge of MacDhonuil Dhu in the house of MacTavish Mhor?'

'She-wolf, be silent with thine ill-omened yell,' answered one of the females, a relation of the deceased, 'and let us do our duty to our beloved kinsman! There shall never be coronach cried, or dirge played, for thee or thy bloody wolf-burd. The ravens shall eat him from the gibbet, and the foxes and wild-cats shall tear thy corpse upon the hill. Cursed be he that would sain your bones, or add a stone to your cairn!'

'Daughter of a foolish mother,' answered the widow of MacTavish Mhor, 'know that the gibbet with which you threaten us is no portion of our inheritance. For thirty years the Black Tree of the Law, whose apples are dead men's bodies, hungered after the beloved husband of my heart; but he died like a brave man, with the sword in his hand, and defrauded it of its hopes and its fruit.'

'So shall it not be with thy child, bloody sorceress,' replied the female mourner, whose passions were as violent as those of Elspat herself. 'The ravens shall tear his fair hair to line their nests, before the sun sinks beneath the Treshornish islands.'

These word recalled to Elspat's mind the whole history of the last three dreadful days. At first, she stood fixed as if the extremity of distress had converted her into stone; but in a minute the pride and violence of her temper, outbraved as she thought herself on her own threshold, enabled her to reply—'Yes, insulting hag, my fair-haired boy may die, but it will not be with a white hand—it has been dyed in the blood of his enemy, in the best blood of a Cameron— remember that; and when you lay your dead in his grave, let it be his best epitaph, that he was killed by Hamish Bean for essaying to lay hands on the son of MacTavish Mhor on his own threshold. Farewell—the shame of defeat, loss, and slaughter remain with the clan that has endured it!'

The relative of the slaughtered Cameron raised her voice in reply; but Elspat, disdaining to continue the objurgation, or perhaps feeling her grief likely to overmaster her power of expressing her resentment, had left the hut, and was walking forth in the bright moonshine.

The females who were arranging the corpse of the slaughtered man hurried from their melancholy labour to look after her tall figure as it glided away among the cliffs. 'I am glad she is gone,' said one of the younger persons who assisted. 'I would as soon dress a corpse when the great fiend himself—God sain us—stood visibly before us, as when Elspat of the Tree is amongst us.—Ay—ay, even overmuch intercourse hath she had with the Enemy in her day.'

'Silly woman,' answered the female who had maintained the dialogue with the departed Elspat, 'thinkest thou that there is a worse fiend on earth, or beneath it, than the pride and fury of an offended woman, like yonder bloody-minded hag? Know that blood has been as familiar to her as the dew to the mountain-daisy. Many and many a brave man has she caused to breathe their last for little wrong they had done to her or theirs. But her hough-sinews are cut, now that her wolf-burd must, like a murderer as he is, make a murderer's end.'

Whilst the women thus discoursed together, as they watched the corpse of Allan Breach Cameron, the unhappy cause of his death pursued her lonely way across the mountain. While she remained within sight of the bothy, she put a strong constraint on herself, that by no alteration of pace or gesture she might afford to her enemies the triumph of calculating the excess of her mental agitation, nay, despair. She stalked, therefore, with a slow rather than a swift step, and, holding herself upright, seemed at once to endure with firmness that woe which was passed, and bid defiance to that which was about to come. But when she was beyond the sight of those who remained in the hut, she could no longer suppress the extremity of her agitation. Drawing her mantle wildly round her, she stopped at the first knoll, and, climbing to its summit, extended her arms up to the bright moon, as if accusing heaven and earth for her misfortunes, and uttered scream on scream, like those of an eagle whose nest has been plundered of her brood. A while she vented her grief in these inarticulate cries, then rushed on her way with a hasty and unequal step, in the vain hope of overtaking the party which was conveying her son a prisoner to Dumbarton. But her strength, superhuman as it seemed, failed her in the trial, nor was it possible for her, with her utmost efforts, to accomplish her purpose.

Yet she pressed onward, with all the speed which her exhausted frame could exert. When food became indispensable, she entered the first cottage: 'Give me to eat,' she said; 'I am the widow of MacTavish Mhor—I am the mother of Hamish MacTavish Bean—give me to eat, that I may once more see my fair-haired son.' Her demand was never refused, though granted in many cases with a kind of struggle between compassion and aversion in some of those to whom she applied, which was in others qualified by fear. The share she had had in occasioning the death of Allan Breack Cameron, which must probably involve that of her own son, was not accurately known; but, from a knowledge of her violent passions and former habits of life, no one doubted that in one way or other she had been the cause of the catastrophe; and Hamish Bean was considered, in the slaughter which he had committed, rather as the instrument than as the accomplice of his mother.

This general opinion of his countrymen was of little service to the unfortunate Hamish. As his captain, Green Colin, understood the manners and habits of his country, he had no difficulty in collecting from Hamish the particulars accompanying his supposed desertion, and the subsequent death of the non-commissioned officer. He felt the utmost compassion for a youth who had thus fallen a victim to the extravagant and fatal fondness of a parent. But he had no excuse to plead which could rescue his unhappy recruit from the doom which military discipline and the award of a court-martial denounced against him for the crime he had committed.

No time had been lost in their proceedings, and as little was interposed betwixt sentence and execution. General ——— had determined to make a severe example of the first deserter who should fall into his power, and here was one who had defended himself by main force, and slain in the affray the officer sent to take him into custody. A fitter subject for punishment could not have occurred, and Hamish was sentenced to immediate execution. All which the interference of his captain in his favour could procure was that he should die a soldier's death; for there had been a purpose of executing him upon the gibbet.

The worthy clergyman of Glenorchy chanced to be at Dumbarton, in attendance upon some church courts, at the time of this catastrophe. He visited his unfortunate parishioner in his dungeon, found him ignorant indeed, but not obstinate, and the answers which he received from him, when conversing on religious topics, were such as induced him doubly to regret that a mind naturally pure and noble should have remained unhappily so wild and uncultivated.

When he ascertained the real character and disposition of the young man, the worthy pastor made deep and painful reflections on his own shyness and timidity, which arising out of the evil fame that attached to the lineage of Hamish, had restrained him from charitably endeavouring to bring this strayed sheep within the great fold. While the good minister blamed his cowardice in times past, which had deterred him from risking his person, to save, perhaps, an immortal soul, he resolved no longer to be governed by such timid counsels, but to endeavour, by application to his officers, to obtain a reprieve, at least, if not a pardon, for the criminal, in whom he felt so unusually interested, at once from his docility of temper and his generosity of disposition.

Accordingly the divine sought out Captain Campbell at the barracks within the garrison. There was a gloomy melancholy on the brow of Green Colin, which was not lessened, but increased, when the clergymen stated his name, quality, and errand. 'You cannot tell me better of the young man than I am disposed to believe,' answered the Highland officer; 'you cannot ask me to do more in his behalf than I am of myself inclined, and have already endeavoured to do. But it is all in vain. General ——— is half a Lowlander, half an Englishman. He has no idea of the high and enthusiastic character which in these mountains often brings exalted virtues in contact with great crimes, which, however, are less offences of the heart than errors of the understanding. I have gone so far as to tell him that in this young man he was putting to death the best and the bravest of my company, where all, or almost all, are good and brave. I explained to him by what strange delusion the culprit's apparent desertion was occasioned, and how little his heart was accessory to the crime which his hand unhappily committed. His answer was, "These are Highland visions, Captain Campbell, as unsatisfactory and vain as those of the second sight. An act of gross desertion may, in any case, be palliated under the plea of intoxication; the murder of an officer may be as easily coloured over with that of temporary insanity. The example must be made, and, if it has fallen on a man otherwise a good recruit, it will have the greater effect."—Such being the General's unalterable purpose,' continued Captain Campbell, with a sigh, 'be it your care, reverend sir, that your penitent prepare by break of day tomorrow for that great change which we shall all one day be subjected to.'

'And for which,' said the clergyman, 'may God prepare us all, as I in my duty will not be wanting to this poor youth.'

Next morning, as the very earliest beams of sunrise saluted the grey towers which crown the summit of that singular and tremendous rock, the soldiers of the new Highland regiment appeared on the parade, within the Castle of Dumbarton, and, having fallen into order, began to move downward by steep staircases and narrow passages towards the external barrier-gate, which is at the very bottom of the rock. The wild wailings of the pibroch were heard at times, interchanged with the drums and fifes, which beat the Dead March.

The unhappy criminal's fate did not, at first, excite that general sympathy in the regiment which would probably have arisen had he been executed for desertion alone. The slaughter of the unfortunate Allan Breack had given a different colour to Hamish's offence; for the deceased was much beloved, and, besides, belonged to a numerous and powerful clan, of whom there were many in the ranks. The unfortunate criminal, on the contrary, was little known to, and scarcely connected with, any of his regimental companions. His father had been, indeed, distinguished for his strength and manhood; but he was of a broken clan, as those names were called who had no chief to lead them to battle.

It would have been almost impossible in another case to have turned out of the ranks of the regiment the party necessary for execution of the sentence; but the six individuals selected for that purpose were friends of the deceased, descended, like him, from the race of MacDhonuil Dhu; and while they prepared for the dismal task which their duty imposed, it was not without a stern feeling of gratified revenge. The leading company of the regiment began now to defile from the barrier-gate, and was followed by the others, each successively moving and halting according to the orders of the adjutant, so as to form three sides of an oblong square, with the ranks faced inwards. The fourth or blank side of the square was closed up by the huge and lofty precipice on which the castle rises. About the centre of the procession, bare-headed, disarmed, and with his hands bound, came the unfortunate victim of military law. He was deadly pale, but his step was firm and his eye as bright as ever. The clergyman walked by his side—the coffin which was to receive his mortal remains was borne before him. The looks of his comrades were still, composed, and solemn. They felt for the youth, whose handsome form and manly yet submissive deportment had, as soon as he was distinctly visible to them, softened the hearts of many, even of some who had been actuated by vindictive feelings.

The coffin destined for the yet living body of Hamish Bean was placed at the bottom of the hollow square, about two yards distant from the foot of the precipice, which rises in that place as steep as a stone wall to the height of three or four hundred feet. Thither the prisoner was also led, the clergyman still continuing by his side, pouring forth exhortations of courage and consolation, to which the youth appeared to listen with respectful devotion. With slow and, it seemed, almost unwilling steps, the firing party entered the square, and were drawn up facing the prisoner, about ten yards distant. The clergyman was now about to retire—'Think, my son,' he said, 'on what I have told you, and let your hope be rested on the anchor which I have given. You will then exchange a short and miserable existence here for a life in which you will experience neither sorrow nor pain.—Is there aught else which you can intrust to me to execute for you?'

The youth looked at his sleeve-buttons. They were of gold, booty perhaps which his father had taken from some English officer during the civil wars. The clergyman disengaged them from his sleeves.

'My mother!' he said with some effort, 'give them to my poor mother!—See her, good father, and teach her what she should think of all this. Tell her Hamish Bean is more glad to die than ever he was to rest after the longest day's hunting. Farewell, sir—farewell!'

The good man could scarce retire from the fatal spot. An officer afforded him the support of his arm. At his last look towards Hamish, he beheld him alive and kneeling on the coffin; the few that were around him had all withdrawn. The fatal word was given, the rock rang sharp to the sound of the discharge, and Hamish, falling forward with a groan, died, it may be supposed, without almost a sense of the passing agony.

Ten or twelve of his own company then came forward, and laid with solemn reverence the remains of their comrade in the coffin, while the Dead March was again struck up, and the several companies, marching in single files, passed the coffin one by one, in order that all might receive from the awful spectacle the warning which it was peculiarly intended to afford. The regiment was then marched off the ground, and reascended the ancient cliff, their music, as usual on such occasions, striking lively strains, as if sorrow, or even deep thought, should as short a while as possible be the tenant of the soldier's bosom.

At the same time the small party which we before mentioned bore the bier of the ill-fated Hamish to his humble grave, in a corner of the churchyard of Dumbarton usually assigned to criminals. Here, amongst the dust of the guilty, lies a youth whose name, had he survived the ruin of the fatal events by which he was hurried into crime, might have adorned the annals of the brave.

The minister of Glenorchy left Dumbarton immediately after he had witnessed the last scene of this melancholy catastrophe. His reason acquiesced in the justice of the sentence, which required blood for blood, and he acknowledged that the vindictive character of his countrymen required to be powerfully restrained by the strong curb of social law. But still he mourned over the individual victim. Who may arraign the bolt of heaven when it bursts among the sons of the forest; yet who can refrain from mourning, when it selects for the object of its blighting aim the fair stem of a young oak, that promised to be the pride of the dell in which it flourished? Musing on these melancholy events, noon found him engaged in the mountain passes, by which he was to return to his still distant home.

Confident in his knowledge of the country, the clergyman had left the main road, to seek one of those shorter paths which are used by pedestrians, or by men, like the minister, mounted on the small but sure-footed, hardy, and sagacious horse of the country. The place which he now traversed was in itself gloomy and desolate, and tradition had added to it the terror of superstition, by affirming it was haunted by an evil spirit, termed *Cloght-dearg,* that is Redmantle, who at all times, but especially at noon and at midnight, traversed the glen, in enmity both to man and the inferior creation, did such evil as her power was permitted to extend to, and afflicted with ghastly terrors those whom she had not licence otherwise to hurt.

The minister of Glenorchy had set his face in opposition to many of these superstitions, which he justly thought were derived from the dark ages of Popery, perhaps even from those of Paganism, and unfit to be entertained or believed by the Christians of an enlightened age. Some of his more attached parishioners considered him as too rash in opposing the ancient faith of their fathers; and, though they honoured the moral intrepidity of their pastor, they could not avoid entertaining and expressing fears that he would one day fall a victim to his temerity, and be torn to pieces in the glen of the Cloght-dearg, or some of those other haunted wilds which he appeared rather to have a pride and pleasure in traversing alone, on the days and hours when the wicked spirits were supposed to have especial power over man and beast.

These legends came across the mind of the clergyman; and solitary as he was, a melancholy smile shaded his cheek, as he thought of the inconsistency of human nature, and reflected how many brave men, whom the yell of the pibroch would have sent headlong against fixed bayonets, as the wild bull rushes on his enemy, might have yet feared to encounter those visionary terrors, which he himself, a man of peace, and in ordinary perils no way remarkable for the firmness of his nerves, was now risking without hesitation.

As he looked around the scene of desolation, he could not but acknowledge, in his own mind, that it was not ill chosen for the haunt of those spirits which are said to delight in solitude and desolation. The glen was so steep and narrow that there was but just room for the meridian sun to dart a few scattered rays upon the gloomy and precarious stream which stole through its recesses, for the most part in silence, but occasionally murmuring sullenly against the rocks and large stones which seemed determined to bar its farther progress. In winter or in the rainy season this small stream was a foaming torrent of the most formidable magnitude, and it was at such periods that it had torn open and laid bare the broad-faced and huge fragments of rock which, at the season of which we speak, hid its course from the eye, and seemed disposed totally to interrupt its course. 'Undoubtedly,' thought the clergyman, 'this mountain rivulet, suddenly swelled by a water-spout or thunderstorm, has often been the cause of those accidents which, happening in the glen called by her name, have been ascribed to the agency of the Cloght-dearg.'

Just as this idea crossed his mind, he heard a female voice exclaim, in a wild and thrilling accent, 'Michael Tyrie— Michael Tyrie!' He looked round in astonishment, and not without some fear. It seemed for an instant as if the Evil Being, whose existence he had disowned, was about to appear for the punishment of his incredulity. This alarm did not hold him more than an instant, nor did it prevent his replying in a firm voice, 'who calls—and where are you?'

'One who journeys in wretchedness, between life and death,' answered the voice; and the speaker, a tall female, appeared from among the fragments of rocks which had concealed her from view.

As she approached more closely, her mantle of bright tartan, in which the red colour much predominated, her stature, the long stride with which she advanced, and the writhen features and wild eyes which were visible under her curch, would have made her no inadequate representative of the spirit which gave name to the valley. But Mr. Tyrie instantly knew her as the Woman of the Tree, the widow of MacTavish Mhor, the now childless mother of Hamish Bean. I am not sure whether the minister would not have endured the visitation of the Cloght-dearg herself, rather than the shock of Elspat's presence, considering her crime and her misery. He drew up his horse instinctively, and stood endeavouring to collect his ideas, while a few paces brought her up to his horse's head.

'Michael Tyrie,' said she, 'the foolish women of the Clachan hold thee as a god—be one to me, and say that my son lives. Say this, and I too will be of thy worship—I will bend my knees on the seventh day in thy house of worship, and thy God shall be my God.'

'Unhappy woman,' replied the clergyman, 'man forms not pactions with his Maker as with a creature of clay like himself. Thinkest thou to chaffer with Him who formed the earth and spread out the heavens, or that thou canst offer aught of homage or devotion that can be worth acceptance in his eyes? He hath asked obedience, not sacrifice; patience under the trials with which he afflicts us, instead of vain bribes, such as man offers to his changeful brother of clay, that he may be moved from his purpose.'

'Be silent, priest!' answered the desperate woman; 'speak not to me the words of thy white book. Elspat's kindred were of those who crossed themselves and knelt when the sacring bell was rung; and she knows that atonement can be made on the altar for deeds done in the field. Elspat had once flocks and herds, goats upon the cliffs, and cattle in the strath. She wore gold around her neck and on her hair— thick twists as those worn by the heroes of old. All these would she have resigned to the priest—all these; and if he wished for the ornaments of a gentle lady, or the sporran of a high chief, though they had been great as MacCallum More himself, MacTavish Mhor would have procured them if Elspat had promised them. Elspat is now poor, and has nothing to give. But the Black Abbot of Inchaffray would have bidden her scourge her shoulders and macerate her feet by pilgrimage, and he would have granted his pardon to her when he saw that her blood had flowed, and that her flesh had been torn. These were the priests who had indeed power even with the most powerful—they threatened the great men of the earth with the word of their mouths, the sentence of their book, the blaze of their torch, the sound of their sacring bell. The mighty bent to their will, and un-loosed at the word of the priests those whom they had bound in their wrath, and set at liberty, unharmed, him whom they had sentenced to death, and for whose blood they had thirsted. These were a powerful race, and might well ask the poor to kneel, since their power could humble the proud. But you!—against whom are ye strong, but against women who have been guilty of folly, and men who never wore sword? The priests of old were like the winter torrent which fills this hollow valley, and rolls these massive rocks against each other as easily as the boy plays with the ball which he casts before him—But you! you do but resemble the summer-stricken stream, which is turned aside by the rushes, and stemmed by a bush of sedges—Woe worth you, for there is no help in you!'

The clergyman was at no loss to conceive that Elspat had lost the Roman Catholic faith without gaining any other, and that she still retained a vague and confused idea of the composition with the priesthood, by confession, alms, and penance, and of their extensive power, which, according to her notion, was adequate, if duly propitiated, even to effecting her son's safety. Compassionating her situation, and allowing for her errors and ignorance, he answered her with mildness.

'Alas, unhappy woman! Would to God I could convince thee as easily where thou oughtest to seek, and art sure to find, consolation, as I can assure you with a single word that were Rome and all her priesthood once more in the plenitude of their power, they could not, for largesse or penance, afford to thy misery an atom of aid or comfort.— Elspat MacTavish, I grieve to tell you the news.'

'I know them without the speech,' said the unhappy woman—'My son is doomed to die.'

'Elspat,' resumed the clergyman, 'he *was* doomed, and the sentence has been executed.'

The hapless mother threw her eyes up to heaven, and uttered a shriek so unlike the voice of a human being, that the eagle which soared in middle air answered it as she would have done the call of her mate.

'It is impossible!' she exclaimed, 'it is impossible! Men do not condemn and kill on the same day! Thou art deceiving me. The people call thee holy—hast thou the heart to tell a mother she has murdered her only child?'

'God knows,' said the priest, the tears falling fast from his eyes, 'that were it in my power I would gladly tell better tidings—But these which I bear are as certain as they are fatal—My own ear heard the death-shot, my own eyes beheld thy son's death—thy son's funeral.—My tongue bears witness to what my ears heard and my eyes saw.'

The wretched female clasped her hands close together, and held them up towards heaven like a sibyl announcing war and desolation, while, in impotent yet frightful rage, she poured forth a tide of the deepest imprecations.—'Base Saxon churl!' she exclaimed, 'vile hypocritical juggler! May the eyes that looked tamely on the death of my fair-haired boy be melted in their sockets with ceaseless tears, shed for those that are nearest and most dear to thee! May the ears that heard his death-knell be dead hereafter to all other sounds save the screech of the raven and the hissing of the adder! May the tongue that tells me of his death and of my own crime be withered in thy mouth—or, better, when thou wouldst pray with thy people, may the Evil One guide it, and give voice to blasphemies instead of blessings, until men shall fly in terror from thy presence, and the thunder of heaven be launched against thy head, and stop for ever thy cursing and accursed voice! Begone, with this malison!— Eslpat will never, never again bestow so many words upon living man.'

She kept her word—from that day the world was to her a wilderness, in which she remained without thought, care, or interest, absorbed in her own grief, indifferent to everything else.

With her mode of life, or rather of existence, the reader is already as far acquainted as I have the power of making him. Of her death I can tell him nothing. It is supposed to have happened several years after she had attracted the attention of my excellent friend Mrs. Bethune Baliol. Her benevolence, which was never satisfied with dropping a sentimental tear when there was room for the operation of effective charity, induced her to make various attempts to alleviate the condition of this most wretched woman. But all her exertions could only render Elspat's means of subsistence less precarious—a circumstance which, though generally interesting even to the most wretched outcasts, seemed to her a matter of total indifference. Every attempt to place any person in her hut to take charge of her miscarried, through the extreme resentment with which she regarded all intrusion on her solitude, or by the timidity of those who had been pitched upon to be inmates with the terrible Woman of the Tree. At length, when Elspat became totally unable (in appearance at least) to turn herself on the wretched settle which served her for a couch, the humanity of Mr. Tyrie's successor sent two women to attend upon the last moments of the solitary, which could not, it was judged, be far distant, and to avert the possibility that she might perish for want of assistance or food, before she sank under the effects of extreme age or mortal malady.

It was on a November evening that the two women appointed for this melancholy purpose arrived at the miserable cottage which we have already described. Its wretched inmate lay stretched upon the bed, and seemed almost already a lifeless corpse, save for the wandering of the fierce dark eyes, which rolled in their sockets in a manner terrible to look upon, and seemed to watch with surprise and indignation the motions of the strangers, as persons whose presence was alike unexpected and unwelcome. They were frightened at her looks; but, assured in each other's company, they kindled a fire, lighted a candle, prepared food, and made other arrangements for the discharge of the duty assigned them.

The assistants agreed they should watch the bedside of the sick person by turns; but about midnight, overcome by fatigue (for they had walked far that morning), both of them fell fast asleep. When they awoke, which was not till after the interval of some hours, the hut was empty, and the patient gone. They rose in terror, and went to the door of the cottage, which was latched as it had been at night. They looked out into the darkness, and called upon their charge by her name. The night-raven screamed from the old oak-tree, the fox howled on the hill, the hoarse waterfall replied with its echoes, but there was no human answer. The terrified women did not dare to make further search till morning should appear; for the sudden disappearance of a creature so frail as Elspat, together with the wild tenor of her history, intimidated them from stirring from the hut. They remained, therefore, in dreadful terror, sometimes thinking they heard her voice without, and, at other times, that sounds of a different description were mingled with the mournful sigh of the night-breeze, or the dash of the cascade. Sometimes, too, the latch rattled, as if some frail and impotent hand were in vain attempting to lift it, and ever and anon they expected the entrance of their terrible patient, animated by supernatural strength, and in the company, perhaps, of some being more dreadful than herself. Morning came at length. They sought brake, rock, and thicket in vain. Two hours after daylight, the minister himself appeared, and, on the report of the watchers, caused the country to be alarmed, and a general and exact search to be made through the whole neighbourhood of the cottage and the oak-tree. But it was all in vain. Elspat MacTavish was never found, whether dead or alive; nor could there ever be traced the slightest circumstance to indicate her fate.

The neighbourhood was divided concerning the cause of her disappearance. The credulous thought that the evil spirit under whose influence she seemed to have acted had carried her away in the body; and there are many who are still unwilling, at untimely hours, to pass the oak-tree, beneath which, as they allege, she may still be seen seated according to her wont. Others less superstitious supposed that had it been possible to search the gulf of the Corrie Dhu, the profound deeps of the lake, or the whelming eddies of the river, the remains of Elspat MacTavish might have been discovered; as nothing was more natural, considering her state of body and mind, than that she should have fallen in by accident, or precipitated herself intentionally into one or other of these places of sure destruction. The clergyman entertained an opinion of his own. He thought that, impatient of the watch which was placed over her, this unhappy woman's instinct had taught her, as it directs various domestic animals, to withdraw herself from the sight of her own race, that the death-struggle might take place in some secret den, where, in all probability, her mortal relics would never meet the eyes of mortals. This species of instinctive feeling seemed to him of a tenor with the whole course of her unhappy life, and most likely to influence her, when it drew to a conclusion.

from *Chronicles of the Canongate* 1827

GLOSSARY

A' all
Abune above
Aff off
Ain own
Amang among
Aneath beneath
Anes once
Aneugh enough
Arles pledges
A'thegether altogether
Awfu' awful
Awn own
Auld old
Aye always

Back-ganging back sliding
Baillie sheriff's officer
Baith both
Banes bones
Banged sprang
Bannocks scones
Barns-breaking frolic
Bating expecting
Belang belong
Bink plate-rack
Birling drinking
Bit little place
Blaud ballad

Blawing blowing
Blink a moment
Blude blood
Blythest happiest
Bogle-wark ghostly work
Bodach spectre
Borrel rustic, rude
Bothy hut, hovel
Braes hills
Brash attack
Breacan Tartan plaid
Brockit white-faced
Brownie ghost
Bye-time past, beyond

Ca'ad called
Caller cooler
Canna cannot
Canny lucky, cunning
Cantrip spell
Carles gruff old men
Carline hag
Cateran freebooter
Cauld cold
Cauld kail repetition
Chaffer chat
Chanter drone of bagpipes
Chiel' fellow

Churl   peasant, boor
Clachan   village
Coronach   lament for the
    dead
Cowped   flopped
Crawing   crowing
Creaghs   raids
Curch   a woman's cap

Daddles   hands
Dang   damn
Dargle   dell
Daur   dare
Daured   dared
Deevil   devil
De'il   devil
Delate   report, inform
Deray   mirthful noise
Didna   did not
Dinna ken   don't know
Dirdum   a mess
Doch-an-dorroch   farewell
    drink
Doddy   without horns
Door-cheek   doorstep
Douce   quiet, sedate
Doun   down
Dour   stern
Dyvour   bankrupt

Eeen   eyes
E'en   even

Fand   found
Fash   trouble

Fasherie   trouble
Faulding   folding
Fause   false
Flitt   to remove
Fou'   full
Frae   from
Freats   superstitious
    notions
Freend   friend

Gae   gave
Gaed   went
Gaen   went
Gang   go
Garr'd   caused
Gash   shrewd
Gaun   going
Gear   property
Ghaist   ghost
Gied   gave
Gien   given
Gillie   man servant
Gin   if, suppose
Girned   grinned, groaned
Graned   groaned
Gratt   cried
Gree'd   agreed
Greishogh   glowing ember
Grit oath   great oath
Grumph   grunt
Grund   ground
Gude   good
Gudesire   grandfather
Gyrecarlin   witch

Hae have
Haill whole
Hail-stanes hailstones
Hame home
Happed hopped
Hauld habitation
Hesp skein of yarn
Het hot
Hieland highland
Himsel himself
Hirdy-girdie topsy-turvy
Hosting assembling troops
Hough-sinews thigh
    sinews
Howlets owls

Ilk each, same, lineage
Ill-faured ill-favoured
Ingle-side fireside
Ither other

Kale-yard cabbage patch
Ken know
Kenn'd known
Keepit kept
Kirkyard churchyard
Kyloes cows

Laith loth
Laird lord
Lang long
Langer longer
Lap leaped
Leal loyal, true
Leesome lane all alone

Lo'es loves
Loon rogue
Loup leap
Lumm chimney

Mair more
Maist most
Mak make
Marcats markets
Maun must
Mear a mare
Merks silver coins
Mickle too much
Mind remember
Miscaad miscalled
Mony many
Moulds graves
Muckle much, great, big
Muhme aunt
Muils slippers
Mutchkin a pint

Nae no
Naebody nobody
Nane none
Needcessity necessity
Neist next

O' out of
O't of it
Ony any
Onywhere anywhere
Ordinar ordinary
Orra other
Ower over

Pairns   children
Parishine   parish
Pick-thank   parasite, low
    fellow
Pock   pouch, bag
Pratty   pretty
Preceese   precise
Puir   poor

Quaig   drinking-cup
Quean   wench
Quotha   forsooth

Raff   worthless person
Raid   rode
Rampauging   roaring
Riped   raked, searched
Rin   run
Roof-tree   roof-beam
Rounds   rungs
Rug   share

Sack-doudling   bagpiping
Sae   so
Sain   bless
Sair   sore
Sangs   songs
Saunt   saint
Saxteen   sixteen
Scauding   scalding
Scowp   bound, caper
Sculduddery   bawdy,
    immoral
Seannachies   chroniclers
Shieling   shelter

Shoon   shoes
Shudge   judge
Sic   such
Siller   silver
Sleekit   smooth
Sneeshing   snuff
Soumons   summons
Spaewife   fortune teller
Speerings   information
Sprack   sprightly
Spule-blade   shoulder
    blade
Stane   stone
Stirk   young steer
Stocking   farm stock
Stots   bullocks
Stoup   flagon, pitcher
Suld   should
Swoln   swollen

Tacksman   tenant
Taen   taken
Tak   taken
Tangs   tongs
Tass   goblet, a glass
Tauld   told
Threap   to insist, aver
Tippeny   twopenny beer
Tod   fox
Toom   empty
Troth   truth
Twa   two

Unca   strange, odd
Usquebaugh   whisky

Wad   would
Walth   wealth
Wame   womb, belly
Wan   want
Wanchancie   unlucky
Warding   awarding
Wared   spent, were
Wark   work
Warld   world
Warst   worst
Wasna   was not
Waur   worst
Weal   welfare

Weel   well
Weel-freended   well-
     friended
Wha   who
Whilk   which
Wi'   with
Wolf-burd   wolf offspring
Wranged   wronged
Wuss   wish

Yelloch   yell
Yetts   gates